THE LORD'S SHARE

THE LORD'S SHARE

Jim Feazell

iUniverse, Inc.
New York Bloomington

The Lord's Share

This is a work of fiction. All of the characters, names, incidents, organizations, and dialogue in this novel are either the products of the author's imagination or are used fictitiously.

iUniverse books may be ordered through booksellers or by contacting:

iUniverse
1663 Liberty Drive
Bloomington, IN 47403
www.iuniverse.com
1-800-Authors (1-800-288-4677)

Because of the dynamic nature of the Internet, any Web addresses or links contained in this book may have changed since publication and may no longer be valid. The views expressed in this work are solely those of the author and do not necessarily reflect the views of the publisher, and the publisher hereby disclaims any responsibility for them.

ISBN: 978-0-595-52762-5 (pbk)
ISBN: 978-0-595-62815-5 (ebk)

Printed in the United States of America

iUniverse rev. date: 6/24/2009

From

JIM FEAZELL
"COME THE SWINE"

An intriguing, spellbinding plot. Eerily believable and frightening. Chuck Abbott, an aspiring young film actor traveled to Heaven, Arkansas in search of his missing Grandfather only to be confronted by a mysterious evil that shrouded the town. For generations the evil had touched the hearts of the townspeople like a contagious disease. No one spoke of it because no one understood it and they feared what they didn't understand. Chuck Abbott was about to learn the horrible truth about the evil. Booger Jim knew about the evil force that permeated the swamp to the north of town and that devil beasts possessed evil souls and that evil begot evil, but then everyone knew Booger Jim was crazy.

Available from iUniverse.com or any online bookseller.
Thanks for your support

From

JIM FEAZELL
"DRY HEAT"

You spend a mind tingling two weeks living
the rigorous enforcement of the law and the
tedious, sometimes futile investigations as
you get to know the officers who serve and
protect the citizens of a crime ridden city.
You will witness the ever growing immorality
of pedophilia. You see a deranged
hematomanian take his bloodlust. You will
visit the mind of a serial killer and learn
why he kills. You tag along with a
schizopherenic psychopath on a multiple
killing spree while staying one step ahead
of the law. And you will feel hurt and deep
sorrow for the Chief losing a young son to
a pederasty.

Available from iUniverse.com, or any
online bookseller.
Thanks for your support.

For Sherry,
This one's for you babe,
Love ya

Forward

On August 1st, 1906, in southwestern Arkansas, diamonds were discovered in a creek bed which later was determined to be the southern edge of a diamond field comprising some seventy-eight acres in size.

This discovery resulted in the only diamonds ever to be found in their natural matrix on the North American Continent. When the discovery became known, a diamond rush started that for awhile was similar to the California gold rush of 1849. For many years since, the site had been shrouded in mystery and legend, splintered by multi-ownerships, cloaked in lawsuits and crippled by lack of funds for mining operations.

In 1972, the discovery site was purchased by the State of Arkansas for use as a state park where visitors now dig for diamonds and keep all they find. Over the years, more than sixty thousand diamonds have been taken from the site. Including some very valuable world famous diamonds such as the; Uncle Sam Diamond (weight 40.42 carats), Star of Murfreesboro Diamond (weight 34.25 carats), Star of Arkansas Diamond (weight 15.31 carats)

The historical event of the 1906 discovery and diamond rush are used in theory only for the basis of the story "The Lord's Share." The entire story in this book is a figment of the authors imagination, and is in no way intended to represent the actual story of the discovery of diamonds in Arkansas.

Chapter 1

Four horses running two abreast were hell bent for leather as they rounded a canyon draw and found flat ground. Two piercing carbine shots rang out in rapid sucession and bounced around the canyon walls like a ricochet symphony. Both outside riders hit the ground.

Later that day a tall man with square jaws and a six-shooter slung low on his hip, walked out of the Marshalls office in Fort Smith counting his money. Tied to the hitching rail beside his big red sorrel were two horses each with a dead man draped across it. Dallas Warbuck supported a reputation among the outlaw element as the most feared bounty hunter of all time. Just to hear his name would cause one to quake in fear.

His profession was honed as a young man before the turn of the century. Across the badlands of New Mexico into the Apache territory of Arizona and back into Texas he pursued his prey relentlessly.

Dallas was a scraggly boy of sixteen when his parents were killed and the farm looted and burned by renegade land grabbers. Much like the Union cavalry regiments known as redlegs some twenty-five years earlier. He had been about four miles from home running mink traps when he returned and found everything gone. He swore over the bodies of his dead parents that he would find those responsible and kill them.

For the next few years he conditioned himself, body and mind, for what he knew he must do, while he hunted down wanted outlaws and collected bounties. It was said that Dallas Warbuck made outlawry a very hazardous occupation.

He searched, and searched, and searched until one Sunday he found them at a political rally in Atlanta. He unwaveringly fulfilled his promise to his parents and himself. Within a matter of seconds he left eight murderous land grabbing villains dead.

After finding out that his Fathers homestead land and all land in a radius of sixty miles belonged to a land leasing corporation called Monticello Farms Development Corporation. He hired an Attorney to find out who the owners of the corporation were. He found that it was owned by a conglomerate of business men with the principle shareholders and officers being eight Union cavalry officers from an old redleg regiment. The attorney found that they would all be at the political rally, where one of them was campaigning in quest of a State office. Being true to their redleg heritage, they all still carried side arms. A blessing for Dallas, he hated to kill an unarmed man. He carried an extra Army Colt in his waistband when he approached them at an outdoor dinner table. When he told them who he was and why he was there, they all jumped up and went for their guns. One of them cleared leather a split second before they were all dead.

Dallas Warbuck felt a great redeeming sense of satisfaction. He had fulfilled his promise to his parents.

It was proven in court that the dead men were indeed the land grabbers and the murderers of a multitude of homestead families. The Judge ruled the killings to be justifiable homicide and Dallas Warbuck was free to continue his chosen occupation of bounty hunting.

He left Atlanta hot on the trail of six wanted outlaws whom he caught up to just south of Memphis, Tennessee. He left two of them with the U.S. Marshal in Memphis, and continued to pursue the other four across Arkansas, where he found them just south of Fort Smith. He left two more dead outlaws with the U.S. Marshal in Fort Smith.

Before leaving town, Warbuck bought some carbine shells and two cans of peachs. He left headed south. The way the other two outlaws, whom he deemed to be the ones known as Pecos and Waco, were going when they lost their companions.

Some eighty or so miles south of Fort Smith looking from atop a natural catback, glorified in all it's splendor, lay a long green grassy valley rimmed by tall pine. A lazy creek meandered through it adorned by tall stands of cottonwood trees. Except for two old prospectors panning in the edge of the creek, the entire valley was void of human life.

"Ain't no gold nowhere round these parts, Jeb. I say we ought'ta head on back out west."

Jeb, was squatted down by the creek sluicing water around in his pan as he watched the trail of black sand. He waited awhile before he answered.

"Yep, guess yer right Farlon, ain't found a color all morning, but I would like to know what these little ol' greasy looking pebbles are though. Ain't never seen nothing like'em afore."

"I'll get ol' Bingo an pack'em up." Farlon said. "We'll go into town and you can find out about them little ol' pebbles."

As Jeb, Farlon and the pack mule began their slow journey up the creek, six wagons emerged from the big pines some four or five miles behind them. They were farm wagons converted for use as covered wagons and had farm implements, chicken coups, water barrels and wash tubs attached to the sides and were pulled by two up teams of horses and mules.

Will and Carrie Summers, from the seat of the first wagon, looked down into the valley.

"Will" Carrie exclaimed. "There's a stream down yonder. Let's stop so's the women can rest up some."

"Looks like good grazing too." Will said. "The hosses sure could use some rest. I reckon we'll make camp, Carrie."

Will shouted ahead to the trail guide as he drew in on the reins.

"Hey Luke—hold up!" Will hollered. From the second wagon, Ollie and Mrs. Fenton saw Luke turn and ride back to the lead wagon.

"Ollie, do you spoze we're go'na stop for awhile?"

"If'n the Lord's willin woman—we'll stop."

Luke turned and started down into the valley. The wagons in turn began following him single file down the slope. A few children ran along beside the wagons playing. Seated on the tailgate of the Summers wagon were fifteen year old Ruth and seventeen year old Clay Summers.

Helen Summers, twenty four year old daughter of Will and Carrie, rode on the tailgate of the Fenton wagon. She jumped down and walked along with her five year old son, Storey. When Storey was a small baby, his father who never packed a gun, was gunned down by a wild drunken cowboy. Helen, a beautiful young farm lady, never remarried or showed any interest in men. Not that they didn't show plenty of interest in her, but she would have nothing to do with any of them. To accentuate her beauty, she had long wavy hair as golden as the late afternoon southwestern sun and deep Robin egg blue eyes, as did all of the Summers children.

The wagons pulled up near the creek and everyone busied themselves with various jobs of setting up camp. The woman in the last wagon gave her milk cow more slack in her rope so she could graze in the tall grass.

The men unhitched the teams and lead them to water. They then took them out into the tall grass and hobbled them. Clay and Ruth gathered firewood and the small kids ran and played.

"Helen!" Carrie yelled. "Gather up all the kids and take'em downstream and give'em a bath."

"Maw, git one of the ladies to help me."

"They're all getting ready to start the cookin' chores."

Luke curried his horse as Will and Clay approached him.

"Hey Luke" Will asked. "How much further you think it might be?"

"Bout ten—maybe twenty weeks."

"Paw." Clay said. "I think we ought to keep movin' on stead'of wastin' time stopping."

Ollie Fenton walked up to them listening as Luke looked around at Clay.

"Best we rest the hosses fer a couple of days." he said. "We got a lot of rough goin' ahead of us."

"Luke's right Clay." Will said. "We'd best rest up some and grease the wagons, so we can make it all the way."

Will Summers was a tall stoop shouldered man that bore the brunt of years of hard work. The deep facial wrinkles and grey hair made him appear much older than his forty-six years.

"Might not be no good farmin' land left time we git there. If'n we ever do." said Clay.

"We'll git there Clay." Ollie said. "The Lord's been with us this far. He'll save us some good land." Ollie Fenton was a small meek man and self proclaimed minister of the Lord. He traveled with the farmers, determined to build his and the Lords church in California.

Two women untied a wooden table from the back of a wagon and took it over to where Carrie and Ruth were cooking. Ruth stirred a large pot of beans over a fire. Carrie, seated on an upside down bucket, fried fatback in a large skillet over another fire.

With the same yellow hair and blue eyes, anyone could readily see that the Summers children took after their mother. Carrie was a beautiful woman as country standards go. Side by side, one would think that she and Helen might be sisters, instead of mother and daughter.

"You men folk come on and eat!" Carrie yelled as she got up and set the skillet on the table. Helen brought some plates and forks to the table. Will, Clay, Ollie, Luke and the other men and women approached the table.

"Carrie, what'cha cook for supper?" asked Will.

"Beans, fatback and pan bread, what else?"

"Same thing we been eatin for the past two months." said Helen.

Ollie helped his plate as if he was starved. "A-Men." he said.

The woman at the last wagon was seated on a stool milking her cow.

Carrie and Helen were waiting plates and the men were finding places to sit and eat. Helen took a bite of beans from a plate on the table. She started to cry and ran away. Mrs. Fenton stood by Carrie with a plate as she waited on some food. "There she goes again, poor child."

"Helen!" Carrie shouted. "You come back here and eat!" She ain't ate enough to keep a cat alive since we left Georgia."

The woman at the last wagon picked up her stool and milk bucket. She went around to the side of the wagon, set them down and returned to the cow to let the slack back out in the rope. Little Storey ran up to the bucket, pulled his overalls down, leaned back, held himself, aimed and urinated in the milk. He looked around to see if anyone was looking as he pulled up his overalls and ran up by the other wagons.

Some distance north of the wagon encampment in mountainous terrain, riding at a fast pace were the two outlaws known as Pecos and Waco. They continually looked behind them, fearing for their lives. Dallas Warbuck, a full day behind them, watched the ground for tracks as he galloped his big red sorrel at a slower pace than the outlaws.

Jeb and Farlon's pack mule had been tied to a hitching rail since daylight. They waited in front of the store with the assayer sign on it until it opened. The town was typical of southern Arkansas at the turn of the century. Most of the buildings were of Gothic design with wood shingle roofs. The sidewalks were wooden with hitching rails in front of the stores. The total make-up of the business section of town was comprised of a town square with a two story courthouse in the center. People were beginning to go about their normal daily routine. The assayer studied Jeb's small pebbles with a jewelers eye glass.

"Where did you find these little rocks?" asked the assayer.

"Bout a full day south." Jeb said. "Whole darn valley full of'em, you ever seen anything like'em?"

The assayer didn't answer. He studied the small pebbles some more at length. A lanky middle-aged man in overalls listened intently to the conversation at the counter as he nonchalantly swept the floor.

"You ever seen anything like'em afore?" Jeb asked again.

The assayer made a scratch test on a hand mirror.

"Only on stick pins and rings."

"What'cha mean?" asked Jeb.

"What I mean is. Ya'll boys have done gone and found some honest to goodness pure bona fide diamonds." Jeb and Farlon stood staring at the assayer in complete astonishment.

The lanky man slowly leaned his broom against the pot-belly stove and went out the door. He looked back momentarily and then broke into a hard run by the mule and into the street directly in the path of an oncoming wagon. The team was spooked and reared up as the tall man fell down trying to avoid them. He got up, regained his posture and hurried on across the courthouse square as the teamster was trying to settle down his team. The tall man went into a mercantile store. The storekeeper was alone putting up stock. "Wes," The man said excitedly. "I need some supplies in a hurry! Shovel—bucket—pans—screen wire! And—and a blanket—and grub! And, oh God—I better get a team and wagon." The man turned to leave and Wes shouted after him.

"Hey, Cooney! Hold up there! How do you figure on paying for all them things?"

Cooney stopped, turned around and approached Wes.

"Wes, you got'ta credit me. You just got'ta. I'll pay'ya in a few days."

"Cooney, you know I can't credit you all of them things. Good Lord, what's done got into you anyway? You done gone plum loco?"

"Wes, I got'ta have'em. You just got'ta let me have'em. Listen Wes" Cooney looked all around to be sure they were alone and spoke secretively.

"Now don't you tell nobody about this. There's done been a strike—a diamond strike. I'll pay'ya twice what the stuff's worth, Wes. I'll be rich in'a few days."

"What are you talking about—a diamond strike?"

"They say they're laying all over the ground. Just laying there, Wes. big as guinea eggs."

"Where?"

"Must be Possum valley. Only'est valley I know of a day south of here."

"Cooney, you must be plum crazy." He pulled off his apron and reached for his hat. "Where you hearing all this nonsense?"

"I done seen'em with my own eyes. The ones what found'em are over yonder in Tom's store right now."

Wes headed for the door leaving Cooney standing in the back of the store.

"Hey, Wes! What about my supplies?" Wes shouted back as he went out the door.

"Help yer'self, Cooney! Help yer'self!"

Wes ran down the street and into the saloon. Momentarily about a dozen men ran out and scurried off in different directions. The news spread through town like wildfire. Within minutes the town was full of people, wagons and teams, all preparing to go to the diamond strike in Possum valley.

Jeb and Farlon came out of the assayer office all smiles and full of jubilance. They slapped each other on the back in a triumphant manner as they pulled the door shut and became immobilized at the chaotic bustling activity about town. A group of men hurried down the sidewalk toward and by them. Farlon addressed one of them.

"What's happenin' out here?"

The man hesitated only long enough to answer. "Haven't ya'll heard? Somebody's done found diamonds down in Possum valley." As the man hurried on, the assayer came out the door with a shovel in his hand and his hat on. He put out his closed sign and hurried down the walk. Jeb and Farlon looked at one another in utter bewilderment.

They knew without a doubt that they had no claim on their discovery and that everybody in the world would be down there scooping up their rightful riches. But nevertheless they must return and salvage what ever they could. They took ol'Bingo and started back to the valley. Farlon noticed Jeb wiping his sweaty face with his bandana.

"No use cryin over spilt milk, Jeb."

Jeb only looked at him contemptuously.

"Where's yer diamonds the assayer had?" asked Farlon.

"They's wrapped up in my bandana." He stopped as he was overcome with a feeling of stupidity.

"No use crying over spilt milk, Jeb."

Ol' Bingo was slow and skidish from all the wagon traffic running by him. They pulled him out away from the trail occasionally to try and settle him down.

Approximately two days to the north, Dallas Warbuck walked slowly while he led his horse. He studied the tracks on the ground and looked around at the lay of the land. The terrain was wooded and hilly. He stood and looked at a river, and by the tracks on the ground he knew they had also been there. It was easy to determine that they had gone down river, undoubtedly looking for a good place to cross.

He reached into his saddlebag and took out a can of peaches, sat on a rock and opened the can with his knife. He drink the juice from the can and then ate the peaches. He mounted the big sorrel and rode down river as he watched for the place where they had crossed. It wasn't long that he found it.

Warbuck pulled off his boots, tied them together with a short leather strap and hung them around his neck. He mounted his horse, waded him into the river and swam across, coming out at the same place as the outlaws. He figured by the signs that he was about one day behind them. Going was slow having to watch for tracks and signs in the rugged terrain, but Warbuck was determined and persistent in his pursuit. He was an expert tracker and he knew his prey would eventually have to stop. His only concern was that they may find a place to stop and set up an ambush for him to ride into. Whenever he saw any such likely place, he would skirt it and pick up the tracks on the other side. If he found no tracks he would know they were back there waiting for him.

This never happened with Pecos and Waco, but it did happen a few years ago when trailing three notorious outlaws through the badlands of New Mexico. He eased back into the small arroyo, coming in behind them. A quick and deadly, close up, hand-gun fight ensued. Two on one side of the arroyo and one on the other fell like pins in a bowling alley.

Warbuck had lambasted the three outlaws for two days, for being so far from a Marshalls office. He lead them, tied across their saddles, south to Las Cruces, the nearest place where there was a U.S. Marshalls office. He collected his bounty and studied the newest posters of other wanted men. He took two posters with him and headed back across southern Texas where these two men would more than likely be. In the Odessa, Big Spring area. It was immaterial to him whether or not he found them. He was at that time headed back to Georgia where a long awaited obligation weighed heavily on his mind.

It was time he looked into keeping a promise he made to his dead parents. He had harbored the deed and doted on it almost nightly since leaving the homestead some dozen years earlier.

Since the deed was effectively taken care of in Atlanta. He had killed four of the six he trailed west across country. And now he was slowly closing in on the other two.

Chapter 2

Bustling activity was the rule of the day for the covered wagon encampment in Possum valley. It was a beautiful sunny morning and everyone was busy. The women washed clothes in the creek. The men worked on wagons. The children ran and played. Will approached a farmer with his wagon propped up and a wheel pulled off. He was stooped down packing grease in the hub.

"Hey there Rufus, you gon'na have that done in time to pull out tomorrow?"

"Ya'll ain't go'na be waitin on me, Will. I'll be done afore the day is over."

Will started to leave and turned back.

"Rufus, tell the madam we preshate ya'll sharin the milk last night, but she sure ought to keep old Betsy out'ta them bitter weeds." Will walked on up to the Fenton wagon. Ollie Fenton was sitting on a cane bottom chair leaned against a wagon wheel, reading his bible.

"Mornin Will, sure is a fine day, ain't it."

"Yeah, sure'nuff is Ollie. One of those days when ya' feel like can't nothin go wrong. Makes a body feel good just to be alive."

On the trail from town to Possum valley was akin to an exodus. A chaotic yet hilariously exciting rush.

(Scott, Foresman   Advanced dictionary) (RUSH; A great or sudden effort of many people to go somewhere or get something.)

The people were going by wagon, buggy, buckboard, saddle horses, mules and many were walking. All carriers were loaded with supplies.

Lil, the saloon owner, Jason Ransom her gambler and her saloon girls were all in a surrey. Behind the surrey was a big wagon loaded with lumber and an upright piano on top. A man pulled at a balking donkey loaded with supplies. The other carriers were passing him by. A wagon loaded down with men carrying shovels hit a bump and bounced some men off. They got up and chased the wagon. Another wagon lost a rear wheel and continued on without it. With visions of riches, these people, come hell or high water, were determined to get to the diamond site.

Ruth admired herself in a mirror propped up on the side of the Summers wagon. Storey came up a short distance behind her, took his pea-shooter from his top overall pocket, put a small pebble in his mouth and shot her posterior. Ruth screamed and started running after him yelling.

"Storey!" You little monster! I'm gon'na pull you bald headed!"

Storey laughed and ran away as Ruth chased him.

She yelled at him "I'm gon'na pull all that yeller hair out'ta yer head!" They ran by Carrie as she placed firewood under a hanging pot. Ruth continued to scream at Storey. Carrie yelled at her.

"Ruth—You leave that child be!—Ruth—you hear me—let that child be!!"

"I'm gon'na kill the little monster if'n I ever catch'em!!!"

On the trail to the strike the wagon that lost the wheel continued on with it's axle dragging. Cooney had loaded a wagon with supplies from Wes's mercantile store and was in the midst of the rush. Wes had another wagon loaded with shovels, wire and lumber. He pulled out right behind Cooney and had stayed in that order. Tom, the assayer, carried only a shovel and went on horseback. Jeb, Farlon and their pack mule were near the back of the rush and were being passed by late starters and stragglers.

Carrie, down on her hands and knees, blew on the coals to get the fire going under the hanging pot. A noisy mass of towns people and wagons were coming down the valley slope toward the creek a ways north of the farmers encampment. Carrie, hearing the commotion, got up and looked. She was utterly flabbergasted. Will, Helen, Clay, Ruth and some of the farmers joined Carrie at the cook pot. All watched in awe at the people and wagons as they continued down the slope. More and more of them converged on the creek, spreading out closer and closer to the farmers wagons. The women started gathering up the children and putting them in the wagons.

"What in tarnations happenin Maw?" asked Ruth.

"Dog'ed if I know." answered Carrie.

"I reckon it'ed be safe to go'an ask." said Will.

"You be careful now Will." said Carrie.

"I'll go with 'ya." said Luke.

"Me too." Clay said. "Let's stay close together."

The farmers walked up the creek a little way to the first group of townsmen digging in the creek bed. Will approached the nearest man.

"What's happen'in? What are all ya'll folks doin?"

"Don't'cha know! There's been a strike on this here creek!"

"Better git'cha a spot whil'est ya'can!"

"What'cha mean a strike."

"Diamonds mister—diamonds!"

Clay and Luke went up the creek and talked to other people who were staking out claims.

"Luke, ya'know what I'm thinking?"

"I reckon I do, Clay—let's go."

The creek was now being overrun with people frantically digging and searching through the gravel and staking claims. Word was passed through the crowd that a claim would be two axe handles long per person. Clay and Luke hurriedly made their way back through the bustling activity to their wagon encampment. The activity had not reached their encampment yet, but was rapidly getting close. Clay quickly got an axe from the wagon and was cutting a four inch sapling as he talked to Luke.

"Luke, I'll drive in this first claim marker. You git one of the ladies to count heads—Count the kids too, and git an axe handle to measure our claims. You're gon'na have to hurry." Clay trimmed and sharpened the claim marker, took a sledge hammer from the wagon and drove the four inch stake into the creek bank even with the front of the Summers wagon, which was parallel to and about forty feet from the creek. He then hurried back to the last wagon. He saw Luke measuring with the axe handle.

"Hey, Clay! Git that other marker cut. We have twenty head. That's forty axe handles. I'll be there in a minute." Clay quickly cut the other stake. Luke finished measuring. It came out just past the last wagon.

"Give it to me, Clay. I'll drive it in."

Will very somberly watched them with a definite feeling of uneasiness. His worry was not because they were staking claims. That only proved the fact that they intended to stay. His worry went much deeper. He worried about being stuck here and not getting to California. Both sides of the creek were lined with people shoveling and washing gravel in all kinds of pans. Various modes of transportation were scattered erratically along the creek with teams still hitched. Will emerged from the far side of his wagon. He watched Clay, Luke and a couple of the other farmers headed down to the creek with shovels, bread pans and skillets. Will's feeling of uneasiness showed on his face. He shook his head back and forth in a depressed manner.

About two hundred yards up the far side of the creek from the farmers wagons. Lil, Jason, the saloon girls and some other men unloaded the piano and lumber. As the driver turned the wagon and left, Lil drew a line with a stick for the saloon front while Jason watched her. Next to Lil's saloon spot, a couple of men unloaded Wes's wagon. Another man was building a floor for a cabin and another putting up a tent.

Some men were building a large sluice box for washing gravel. Another man was snaking a log down the slope with a team of mules. Will stood on the creek bank and watched Clay, Luke and one of the farmers crudely scratching through gravel in pans looking for diamonds.

"Clay, git out'ta that creek a'fore you take sick. Yer ruinin yer Maw's cookin' pan."

Clay kept on working at his gravel, pretending not to hear Will.

"Come on Will." The farmer said. " They say there's diamonds here."

"What do ya'll know bout diggin diamonds?" Will said. "All ya'll know is diggin' taters. Ya'll don't even know what diamonds look like. Now git out'ta there, we got work to do, so's we can move on ta'California."

"Will" Luke said. "I ain't a'goin on ta'California long as I can git diamonds from this here creek."

"What do'ya mean you ain't goin on, Luke! We all paid you to guide us! You got'ta do it!"

"Now simmer down Will, I'll give ya'lls money back. Anyway, I don't think nobody else is wantin to go on."

"Aw, come on Paw, git'cha a pan, they say we can git rich here."

"Rich!—rich!—what the hell's rich?—Gittin yer butt wet playin in that creek!"

Will turned and walked away disgustedly shaking his head.

"Guess I'll move downstream a ways." Clay said. "And find me a good spot."   Clay was experiencing mixed emotions about going against his father's wishes. He could not remember ever doing that before and he felt like he needed to be alone.

Beside the wagon with the chicken coops, Carrie and Helen fed and watered the hens as Storey played with the rooster in another coop. He would stick his finger through the wire and jerk it back while he made faces at the rooster.

"Maw, what's gon'na happen now. With everybody gone off down there huntin' diamonds?" asked Helen.

"I don't rightly know. Maybe yer Paw can talk to'em." Will overheard the conversation as he walked up to them.

"I've tried already, Carrie, but I don't reckon it's helped none. They all seem'ta be touched with some kind'a fever bout finding diamonds, and our boy Clay is as bad as any one of'em."

Helen started to cry. "I wish we hadn't never left home."

"Now Helen." Carrie said. "Don't start that again, you know we all agreed, things are go'na be a whole lots better out in California."

"But are we go'na ever git there?" Helen ran off crying.

"Maybe she's right Carrie. Least we had a roof over our heads back home."

Dallas Warbuck got off his horse and led him for a way while he studied the tracks. He then mounted his horse and rode at a slow gallop while he continued to watch the ground.

Pecos and Waco, in fear of the bounty hunter, constantly looked behind them. They still rode at a faster pace than Warbuck. Warbuck realized that as he studied the tracks, and he also realized that they would soon have to stop. If not for their own sake—for the sake of the horses.

Will and Carrie sat in the chairs by the wagon and contemplated their situation wondering how to rectify it. They knew there were only three choices, Turn around and go back to Georgia where they would have to find a share-cropping farm where it would be next to impossible to make a living, even if they could find one. Or, try to figure out how to continue on to California without a trail guide. Or, stay here in this God forsaken hell hole. The latter not even being a consideration.

"Will." Carrie asked. "Do you think we might could git there without a guide."

" Naugh, we'd probely git off on the wrong trail and git lost. Maybe wind up in Indian country or somethin."

"Then our only salvation is to find us a guide." Carrie said.

"I'll start askin round again." Will said. "If'n we were ta'find somebody. I still don't know what ta'do bout Clay."

"Maybe we could all jump'em, hog-tie'em and put'em in the wagon." Will looked at her curiously trying to understand if she was serious. She dropped her face into her hands and began to sob. Will got up and put his arms around her affectionately.

"There, there, Carrie, it'll be alright, don't you worry yourself. I'll think of something. Right now, I think I'll go an talk to Luke some more." He went down the creek leaving Carrie wiping her face on her apron. Luke was working only a short distance down the creek from the Summers wagon. He was on the bank making coffee when Will approached him.

"Hey Luke, ya'findin any diamonds?"

"I'm doin pretty good, Will."

"Ya'know Luke, you're obligated'ta guide us on'ta California, whether ya'want to or not. It's yer Christian duty to keep yer promise. A sacred promise is just as bindin as a written contract."

"That's a good little speech Will, but I don't know how to tell you any plainer that I'm not leavin here." Will just looked at him knowing it was fruitless and not knowing what else to say.

"Alright then Luke, give me back the money we all paid'ya, like ya'said you would. We need it ta'try ta'find somebody else ta'guide us."

Luke looked expressionless at Will for a long while before speaking.

"What do you think you might do if'n I don't give it ta'ya."

Will answered seriously. "I reckon I'll go git my shotgun an come back an shoot'ya."

"Will, you're not the kind of man what would kill somebody."

"Maybe not Luke, but I wouldn't think twice bout shootin' off yer knee caps."

Luke saw the determined seriousness in Will's face. He stood up and unbuttoned his shirt pocket, took out some money, and counted out three hundred dollars. He handed it to Will and started to say something.

"All of it." said Will.

Luke handed him two more hundred. Nothing else was said. Will, turned and left going back to the wagon.

Will gave Carrie the money to put up and told her he was going to search for a guide. He waded across the creek to where some men were unloading lumber and starting to build a store. He talked to numerous men about being a wagon train guide. Most would not even listen to him. Those that did only laughed at him and wished him luck, or thought him crazy for wanting to leave the diamond site.

Feeling sad and depressed, he went back to the wagon and told Carrie the bad news.

"Don't let it git you down, Will." Carrie said in a consoling manner. Somethin' will come up so's we can go on. Let's just give it some time an do some prayin bout it. I don't want ya ta'make yerself sick worry'in bout it."

Helen and Storey appeared from a walk out in the field leading up to the valley slope.

"Granma, I'm hungry." said Storey.

"Guess I better start fixin some dinner." said Helen.

"You build the fire." Carrie said. "I'll start the dinner."

"I'm go'na lay down awhile." Will said. "Let me know when it's ready."

Carrie watched Will climb up into the wagon.

"Just as I suspected," she told Helen. "Yer Paw's done took sick over this diamond strike holding us up. He never goes to bed this time of day, specially afore supper."

"What we gon'na do now, Mama?"

"I don't rightly know, child."

"I wish we hadn't never left Georgia." Helen sobbed.

"Don't start that now, you're go'na make yerself sick too. An I need ya ta'help me. I wish we hadn't left too, but we did and there's no undoin it now. We all just got ta'buckle down and make the best of it. Yer Paw will figure something out. He'll find a way to get us back on the trail to Califirnia."

Helen wiped her eyes and with her bottom lip trembling she looked pitifully at Carrie. She started putting some kindling sticks in the fire hole to start the fire. Carrie unwrapped some left over pan bread for Storey to eat on while supper was being cooked.

They were simple, modest and loving country folk, who wanted only to better their stance in life. Life on the Georgia homestead had gotten intolerably poor. They could not sell a crop or save enough seed to grow food. They knew it would only worsen since the Union reconstruction had repealed all homestead rights. Will and Carrie attended meetings with other farmers and talked of hearing about how California was welcoming homesteaders to come there where there was ample rich farm land begging to be farmed. It sounded like Utopia. Who wouldn't want to go? Will organized the wagon train of six families and left on the long journey.

Chapter 3

There are those that would much rather take advantage of a situation like the diamond rush to make a financial killing by applying their own profession or trade to the outcome. Those people had worked day and night for days getting ready to make their fair share of the wealth coming from the creek. The beautiful serene valley was no more.

On the morning of the fourth day a so called town had emerged along the creek. The busy <u>main street</u> as it had already been dubbed ran parallel to, and about fifty feet from the creek, across and up the creek a little way from the farmers wagons. The business establishments were all on the side of the street away from the creek.

By the fifth morning there was a completely constructed mercantile store with two men nailing shingles on the roof. There were barrels of items in the front with price signs on them and Wes putting a price sign on some rolls of screen wire. On the south side of the mercantile store some men hammered and sawed on another almost completed building and two men hung a big "café" sign above the door. To the south of the café was Lil's saloon. The saloon was fairly large with a wooden floor. It had wooden sides up about halfway with a large canvas top across rafters. To help secure the saloon top, Jason pulled on a guy rope and tied it off to a stake in the ground. Connected to the side of the saloon was another large canvas tent. Lil walked out of it to inspect the saloon. Down the road a ways, south of Lil's saloon a Chinaman had hung a "bath house" sign by a clapboard wall. Inside of a square of such walls were three huge iron washtubs for boiling water and four number three size wash tubs strategic placed in each corner with blankets hung for privacy. To the south of the bath house a blacksmith had just shod his first horse at a newly constructed blacksmith shop, complete with sign and horse corral. There were many canvas tents and clapboard shanties strung along the slope behind the business's and down along the winding creek. The area bustled with activity. Wagons and horseback riders going up and down the street and people hard at work on the construction of other establishments along Main street.

Ruth stood at the far end of the newly developed town and looked at it in a state of delightful wonderment.

Will, with a wretched feeling of foreboding anxiety, emerged from the back of his wagon and approached the Fenton wagon where he found Ollie sitting on a cane bottom chair reading his bible.

"It sure is good to see that you ain't went and gone diamond crazy like the rest, Ollie. What'cha spoze we go'na do now?"

"What'cha mean, Will?"

"I mean it looks like we're the only'est sane ones left, and we've been stuck here nigh on to bout a week now."

"Stuck here?"

"We sure can't go on with just two wagons and no trail guide."

"Maybe if'n you'd talk to'em some more."

"Naugh, they's past talkin to, unless…" Will, inspired with a brilliant idea, perked up. "Yeah, Ollie, maybe they'd listen to you. Whyn't you try talkin' some sense in to'em. Remind'em bout all that good farmin land out there in California, just sittin there waitin fer us!"

"Alright Will, tonight after everbody's ate supper. I'll talk to'em, I'll read'em a few scriptures of gospel too."

"Lord knows, they sure need it, Ollie."

"A-Men!"

Carrie was pleased to see Will up and about. She had been frightfully concerned about him. She had taken him food into the wagon and made him eat.

Jeb, Farlon and a large man with a short cropped black beard were working close together in the edge of the creek. They were washing gravel and scratching through it in their gold pans. Jeb, picked out a small diamond and put it in his pouch. The big man moved over closer to him.

"Arn't ya'll the ones what made this here strike?"

"That's right." Jeb said. "We sure' nuff are."

"Mighty decent of ya'll to share yer good fortune."

"Twarn't our intentions."

"The Lord will bless'ya fer it."

"You be some kind'a preacher mister?"

"I been called. Name's Jules Blackburn. Soon's I heared bout this here strike, the Lord told me to git on out here and keep the fear of God in these peoples hearts—Ya'll God fearin men?"

"Naugh." Farlon said. "We're whiskey fearin men."

Farlon reached in his back pocket and took out a bottle. He uncorked it and handed it toward Blackburn.

"Have a snort, Preacher." he said egotistically.

Blackburn unhesitatingly reached for the bottle. He took it quickly, looked at it admirably and gently wiped the top with his shirt sleeve as he spoke.

"Only'est way I've ever found to keep my throat clear, so's to do a better job for the Lord."

He turned the bottle up and guzzled down the most part of it. Jeb and Farlon looked at him in disbelief.

Beside the Summers wagon, Carrie and Helen had taken some more dried beans out of the food cupboard on the side of the wagon. They kept beans cooking almost constantly because of the time involved in cooking them. Ruth, at the mirror, had taken down her pig-tails and was brushing out her hair, Carrie saw Will as he approached them.

"You seen anything of Clay today?" she asked.

"I spoze he's on the creek, like everbody else."

"How come we don't just hitch up and go on by ourselves?"

"We'd never make it by ourselves, cause we don't know the way. Ollie's gon'na talk to the rest of 'em tonight. Maybe they'll listen ta' him."

Helen covered her face with her apron and began to cry. Ruth laid the hair brush down and left.

"I wish we'd never left home." Helen sobbed. "I wish we was—."

"Awe, dad-gum it, Helen, hush up." Will stammered. "We got trouble enough without all that bawlin."

With Lil's directions, Jason had problems hanging a sign straight over the saloon. Lil exasperated, gave up and went into the saloon. The sign read in bold red letters "DIAMOND LIL'S" with smaller letters under it which said. "we buy diamonds" Jason secured the sign at an angle. He started down the ladder and saw Ruth watching him. "Hello there, pretty lady. Who are you?" Ruth turned and looked for someone else and turned back to look at him. "Who me?" "I'm just Ruth Summers."

"Well now, I'm right pleased to make your acquaintance, Miss Summers. My name is Jason Ransom."

"You sure do talk pretty."

"And you sure do look pretty. Where are you from?"

"I'm from over yonder at them wagons across the creek. We're movin' ta'California."

"Well, I sure hope them wagons don't get in no big hurry to leave, not when I've just met such a lovely young lady."

Ruth blushed, smiled and turned away. She turned back and looked at him on the ladder. "I've got to go now." she said.

"You be sure and come see me again now, you hear."

She walked over to the creek and across the walk bridge which Lil had paid some men to construct. Lil wanted to make it as convenient as possible for the diamond seekers to get to her saloon.

As Ollie Fenton walked along the creek bank. He stopped and watched Jules Blackburn, Jeb and Farlon wash and search gravel in their pans as they stood in half knee deep water. Farlon noticed Ollie's bible in his hand.

"Glory be, we got us two preachers."

"You be a worker for the Lord, brother?" Jules asked.

"Name's Ollie Fenton. I'm with the wagons what's tryin ta'go on ta'California. Go'na build me an the Lord a church there."

"You don't look ta'be man enough to put the fear of God in nobody. I'm Reverend Jules Blackburn. The Lord has saw fit to put me here to git his fair share of the diamonds from this strike."

" I'm havin a sermon tonight at the wagons." Ollie said. "Be mighty pleased to have ya'll there."

"Kind of you to ask, Brother Ollie, I'll shur be there."

Ollie acknowledged Jules acceptance with a smile and went on up the creek. Farlon took his bottle out of his pocket. Jules hastily reached for it. Farlon turned away and took a fast drink, corked the bottle and put it back in his pocket.

During supper time at the wagon encampment, everyone talked about and looked forward to hearing Ollie preach. As it approached dark most of the people had gathered for the sermon. All of the farmers including women and children were there. Some of the men made a small campfire and others brought lanterns. Jules Blackburn, Jeb and Farlon sat on the ground close to Ollie, Mrs Fenton, Will and Carrie Summers. Helen and Ruth were sitting by the campfire with the children. It was getting dark and men were lighting the lanterns. Ollie got up and stepped up to a rough-hewn homemade rostrum and laid his bible on it. Someone put a lighted lantern on the rostrum beside the bible. Ollie raised his arms to get everyone's attention.

"Brothers and Sisters, we are gathered together again in the presence…" The noise level got much higher from the saloon. A honkytonk piano, girls laughing and screaming, Men whooping and hollering. It was so loud it drowned Ollie out. He tried again as loud as he could.

"…In the presence of the Lord!!—There is much of great importance to be."

The saloon noise again drowned him out. Through a few cottonwood trees and up the creek to the other side could be seen many lanterns hanging from poles and men scurrying about in the lantern light going in and out of the saloon. The noise was not letting up. Jeb, Farlon and a farmer slipped off toward the saloon. Ollie tried again.

"There is much of great importance to be!!!"

The noise was to much for Ollie. More of the farmers were stealing away toward the saloon. Story got up and started to follow them. Helen grabbed him and made him set down as Jules shouted at Ollie.

"Louder   brother   Ollie!   Tell'em   they're sinners!!"

"Folks !!!' Ollie tried again. "I know the distraction is !!!"

The noise from the saloon seemed to pick up in volume and drowned Ollie out again." "He yelled as loud as he could."

"If'n ya'll will come back and listen!!! I'll—I'll try'ta !!!."

The noise got the best of him. He gave up and sat back down by Mrs. Fenton, Will and Carrie.

"I'm sorry Will, they just don't want to listen to me, with all that is goin on over yonder."

"I know Ollie, they ain't never seen that kind of excitement a'fore, it's just to much fer'em."

"Ain't yer fault, Ollie." said Carrie.

Most of what was left of Ollie's congregation got up and went to the wagons. Jules Blackburn walked away mumbling incoherently about how they are all sinners and are going to burn in hell. The saloon was quite crowded with miners, prospectors, and farmers which left the wagon encampment, and Ollie's would be sermon.

The saloon had a long bar and many tables and chairs. The saloon girls kept the excitement going, drinking and dancing with the customers.

Lil sat at the end of the bar under a large sign which read "Sell your diamonds here" She had a cash box and looked at the diamonds with a jewelers eye glass. She would pay ten dollars for a small diamond. Twenty dollars for a medium one and thirty dollars for a big one. Small diamonds were about the size of an okra seed. Medium ones about the size of buckshot. A large diamond, about the size of a black eye pea. And quite rarely there would be a diamond that brought everyone running to see it. An extremely large one ranged in size from a chinquapin to a hickory nut. That's when Lil would have to break out some hundred dollar gold pieces and haggle the price. She bought them by physical size instead of carat. The man that drove Lil's supply wagon ran the chuck-a-luck game. Jason Ransom ran a crooked roulette wheel and the typical piano player with the derby hat and garters on his sleeves kept the loud honkytonk music going.

Ruth watched the excitement through a small opening in the side wall of the saloon. She had never seen anything to equal the excitement. She was more than amazed at the beautiful clothes the ladies wore, and the fun they were having. In her young mind it was beyond all reality. She wanted to stay longer but knew she better get back to the wagon. As she went across the bridge she preconceived a notion to ask Jason about working there and had mental reflections of wearing one of those pretty dresses. The thought of sitting on a mans lap and having a drink gave her a hormonal rush that excited and scared her. She hurried to get to the encampment. The few that was left were sitting around drinking coffee and talking. Coffee was a big thing with country folk. It took away the inhibitions and relaxed them. They all drink it. Ruth went to the pot and got her a plate of beans and broke off some bread. As she sat down, Carrie watched her every move with concern and wondered where she had been. She deduced by motherly reasoning that she should start keeping a shorter leash on her.

"Will." Carrie said. "Bein as how Brother Ollie is here. How bout us holdin a special prayer service afore we turn in. An pray bout the predicament we're in what's keepin us from goin on ta'California. Brother Ollie, would you be so kind as to lead us in prayer?"

"Sister Carrie, it would be my most grateful pleasure. Let's all gather round real close so's the noise from that unrighteous den of iniquity don't drown me out."

"A-Men." said Mrs. Fenton.

"Ollie" Will said. "Be sure an tell'em how they should cut out this here diamond foolishness and get back on the trail ta'California. Tell'em we need ta'git on out there an start puttin crops in the fields."

"I'll tell'em Will."

"A-Men." said Mrs. Fenton.

Chapter 4

The hectic activity along the creek continued as more people came in search of riches. Lil and Jason stood in front of the saloon watching the new arrivals. "We bought some fine diamonds last night, Jason." Lil said. "I've got to keep them selling their diamonds to me. They'll do it too, long as I can keep'em happy at night."

"What do you mean, Lil?"

"Looks like we might have to enlarge the saloon. And more girls, we need more girls. Jason, I want all the diamonds I can get from here before this strike plays out. And I'll get them any way I can. You see to it, you hear."

Lil went into the saloon. Jason stood there in somewhat of a confounded state talking to himself. He spoke aloud in an antagonistic attitude, as if he were talking to Lil, but knowing she was not hearing him.

"Just how am I going to enlarge the saloon when there is no room on either side? And just where am I supposed to find more girls in a place where there aren't any girls?"

Ollie Fenton sat on the creek bank and watched Jules Blackburn dig and wash gravel. Clay Summers worked a few feet downstream from Jules. Clay and Luke did not get all the claims they staked out. The other miners would not let them have claims for the women and children.

"Brother Ollie, I know the Lord put me here to git his share of the diamonds. Jules said, as he looked at Ollie on the bank. "Looks like so far he ain't wantin much of a share."

"Gol—lee!" Exclaimed Clay. Hey, Ollie! Look at the size of this one!"

Clay excitedly picked the diamond from his pan as Ollie stepped up to the edge of the water to look at it. "You hit a good pocket there, did'ya Clay?" asked Jules.

Jules started working closer and closer to Clay's hole as Clay went to the bank to show the diamond to Ollie. He wound up in Clay's hole and was frantically filling his pan with gravel.

"Looks like a little ol' grey rock to me." Ollie said. Clay looked around and saw Jules in his hole.

"Come on now Jules! Git back over in yer own hole! Git out'ta mine!"

"Now son, you wouldn't begrudge just one little one fer the work of the Lord, would you?"

"Git, I said! Git out!"

Jules Blackburn retreated to his own diggings mumbling. He took a bottle from his pocket and took a big drink. As he put his bottle back into his pocket he saw two horseback riders coming down the valley slope. They reined up across the creek from Ollie, by Clay and Jules. Enter Pecos and Waco.

"Morn'in." Pecos said.

"Morn'in." answered Jules.

"Findin any gold here?"

"Naugh," Jules said seriously. "Ain't no gold here."

"There a town nearby?" Waco asked.

"Somewhat'a one right there." Jules pointed. "Bigger one bout ten miles north."

"Thank'ya friend." Pecos said.

Pecos and Waco rode up toward the blacksmith shop.

"Who were they, Brother Jules?"

"Never seen'em afore, but I've seen plenty of their kind. Hope they keep movin. Be trouble round here if'n they stay."

Pecos and Waco passed the blacksmith shop and rode on up Main street looking intently at the people working the creek. They stopped at Diamond Lil's, dismounted and tied their horses to the hitching rail. Pecos saw Jason come out of the saloon.

"Jason?" Jason Ransom. Is that really you? It's been a long time."

"Pecos?" Jason answered. "Yeah, it's been at least three years. I thought you would'of been hung by now. What are you doin in these parts? Don't tell me you're gon'na dig for diamonds? You never worked a day in your life."

"Diamonds? This ain't no gold strike?"

"Nope, this one's different, it's for diamonds. Say, why don't you try your luck, or, are you just passing through? I mean, well, you know, on the run, maybe?"

"Yeah, Jason, something like that. Kind'a the same way you left Texas, if I recollect right. Me and Waco here, we, oh—this here's Waco."

Pleased to meet you." Jason said.

"Howdy."

"As I was sayin, me and Waco, we went and got us a little price on our heads. So we had to move on. A while back we learn't that there's this bounty hunter trailin us. He shot four of our partners. Like to of had us twice, but we give'em the slip."

"Just one man? And there were six of you? Couldn't you handle him?"

"Not this man." Waco said. "He's collected more bounties than anybody I ever heard of. I'm all fer runnin.'"

"Yeah." Pecos said. "We don't care to tangle with nobody what's as fast with a gun as he is. He's a persistent cuss too. We had a bank robbery to go rotten in a little town just west of Atlanta and a couple of bankers were killed. He was on our trail before we knew it. There were six of us and he killed two of our partners near Memphis and then two more near Fort Smith.

"Who is this bounter hunter? What's he called?" Jason asked.

"He's called Warbuck." Pecos said. "Dallas Warbuck."

"Dallas Warbuck! Yeah, I've heard of him. You know, Pecos, this could be just the place for you boys to lay low for awhile. Why don't you go downstream and wash gravel for a few days? And get'ya some diamonds. If anybody looks like Warbuck shows, I'll come and let you know."

"I don't know if that's such a good idea." Waco said.

"I'd sure like to find one of those diamonds." Pecos said.

"I'll buy the diamonds you find." Jason said. "And you want have to worry about that bounty hunter sneaking up on you either."

True to Jasons character, the crooked wheels in his head were conceiving ulterior motives as they talked. He needed to get Pecos and Waco to stay. He knew if he ever was going to make a killing and get out from under Lils control he would need someone to do his biding. And they would be perfect. He looked over and saw Ruth watching him from the corner of the saloon.

"Stake us to a shovel and some grub?" Pecos asked.

"Get what you need at the store and charge it to me."

Jason walked over to see Ruth.

"Hello, pretty lady, did you come by to brighten my day?"

"I guess so." Ruth said with a smile.

"Well you sure do. You're as pretty and bright as the morning sun."

Jason looked her over with an amorously desiring disposition.

"Has anyone ever told you how pretty you are?"

"No, I don't reckon." she said, as she blushed.

Carrie approached Helen as she stirred the big cooking pot.

"Helen, you seen anything of Ruth?"

"No Maw, not fer awhile."

Carrie walked up the creek and searched through the people. She saw Ruth and Jason in front of the saloon and crossed the bridge fuming with anger but did not let it show. She knew she was going to have trouble with Ruth. She was of that age to start noticing men. Carrie didn't know what to do and she was scared for Ruth. She approached them and took Ruth by the arm. She started to pull her away as Jason meekly walked away and went down the street.

"Ruth, you come with me, right now." Carrie, without any resistance, pulled Ruth across the walk bridge and toward the wagons.

"Aw Maw, we was just talkin."

"What's that man talking to you bout? I want you to stay away from him. You hear me."

"But Maw, we was just talkin bout how he could help me."

"Help you—how? What do you mean?"

"Help me to do my part fer the family. He said he would give me a job at the saloon. He said he would take care of me Maw, he likes me, he told me so. Jason's a nice man, Maw."

Helen sat outside the wagon reading to Storey.

"Ruth, you stay with your sister, I'll be back directly, and I mean you stay here!"

Ruth had never felt so depressed or dejected. She was totally confused as she walked around kicking at stones and watched her mother going back toward the saloon.

"Ruth, come over here and sit down." Helen said. "Tell me what's happened."

Lil, a robust middle aged lady, with a bee hive hair do, a bright red, low cut long dress and looking like the typical saloon madam, sat at the counter checking a diamond. She looked up as Carrie came through the door.

"Hello there, you must be one of the ladies from the wagon camp. Can I help you?"

"You the one called Lil, what owns this place?"

"Yes?"

"Well, I'm Carrie Summers, and I'm here to tell you to see that your husband don't go botherin my girl Ruth no more. She's just a young'un and don't know nothin bout no man moonin over her. And further more, I don't want her workin in no such place as this."

"Hold on, Mrs. Summers. Now slowdown. Who do you mean, my husband? I've got no husband."

"You know who I mean—that—that Jason man—he's—ain't he your husband?"

"I believe I'm beginning to see now. No, Mrs. Summers, he's not my husband. But I'll see that he stays away from your girl, you leave it to me, and don't worry anymore about it."

Jason entered as Carrie left. He looked back at her as she went out the door. He then looked at Lil and turned to go back out.

"Jason! Get over here!"

Jason reluctantly moved closer to Lil.

"What is it? What was that woman doing here?"

"You know dad-gum well what that woman was doing here! Jason you are undoubtly the biggest idiot I've ever known. Here we have a chance of getting rich, and you want to ruin it all over some little farm girl. If I ever hear of you being near her again, I'm through with you. You will be on your own."

"But Lil, you said you needed more girls."

"Yes, saloon girls. Not farm girls, and especially not children! And not for your personal pleasure either! Now get out of my sight. I don't want to see you before working time tonight. And Jason, you better hope that girls Paw don't hear of this. Them kind of people take a very dim view of such goings on."

Jason looked very worried and turned and left. In an outburst of mental anguish as he went out the doorway, he kicked the tent causing the sign to fall and hit him on the foot. He fell to the ground and held his foot for awhile before he got up and limped away.

When Carrie returned to the wagon, Ruth was putting firewood under the cooking pot. Will, seated by the wagon, immediately noticed the stearn looks between Carrie and Ruth.

"What's a matter with you two." Will asked.

"Nothin to git concerned bout. Just a little spat." Carrie answered.

Pecos and Waco were sitting beside the stream on the far south end of the existing claims as new prospectors were showing up. They had staked them a claim, but were doing nothing.

"I'm not so sure this is a good idea." Waco said. "I'm thinking it might be best if we rode on."

"Might as well for all the good we're doin." Pecos said. "We'd have ta'git in the water ta'find a diamond. Like them other people are doin."

Jason walked up and Waco excitedly jumped up.

"Is he here Jason? Is he here?"

"Relax Waco, that's not what I'm here for. How you doing. Found any diamonds yet?"

"Naugh." Pecos said. "We're not doin no good, just not much cut out for this kind of work."

"We couldn't even buy beans yet." Waco said.

"Don't worry about it boys, I've got a plan that will make us all rich."

"We're listening Jason." Pecos said.

"It's very simple. I want to take over Lil's place. It's going to take in over half the diamonds coming out of this creek."

"How you intending on doing that?" Pecos asked.

"I sure ain't killing no woman!" Waco said.

"You won't have to kill anyone. I'll just need your help when the time comes."

"Jason, are you forgetting about that bounty man?" Pecos asked.

"No, I'm not forgetting. You boys work for me and I'll take care of your bounty man."

"How Jason?" Waco asked. "He's fast, and you don't even pack a gun."

"Leave that to me. If he shows, I'll buy him off. How much is on your heads?"

"Five hundred each." Pecos said.

"Yeah." Waco said. "Two of us—that's—a thousand?" He looked at Pecos for assurance. Pecos nodded at him.

"Yeah." Waco said haughtily. "A thousand."

"Hope you boys are worth it. It a deal?"

Pecos and Waco looked at one another.

"It's a deal" Pecos said. "You take care of Warbuck, and we work for you." Jason turned to leave and then turned back to Pecos.

"Oh, by the way. There's a farmer you may have to take care of for me later."

Jason turned and walked away.

A few miners stood and watched Clay work and pick out diamonds from his pan. Jason stopped and watched for a while and then continued toward the saloon. He moved slowly along the creek across from the wagon encampment, looking across to see if he could spot Ruth. There were people scurrying about, but he didn't see her. After passing the livery stable and bath house, he went behind the business's and up the slope to his small tent. He crawled into the tent to take a nap. He did not want to see Lil before working time.

During the time of the pursuit south through Arkansas, the terrain had leveled off to rolling hills and small valleys as Dallas Warbuck, still a day behind Pecos and Waco, picked up the pace. The tracks had became easier to follow. And he knew he was gaining on them. He also knew they were trying to throw him off their trail by zig zagging across country and making long and wide circles crossing their own trail in an attempt to lose him. Pecos and Waco were crafty, but not crafty enough to elude Warbuck. They had traveled southeast and bypassed the town where the rush had commenced. They then had turned back west and down into the valley of diamonds. Even after all of the problems of trying to confuse Warbuck, they were skeptical of it working and continued to look behind them. They contemplated stopping and trying to ambush him, but dismissed the notion due to extreme fear. Running into Jason Ransom, they surmised, was a real streak of luck and a welcomed reprieve from worry—providing he buys Warbuck off like he said. It never occurred to them that he may not. Honor among thieves—you know.

Pecos and Waco, leaned back on their saddles and watched the creek, occasionally glancing at one another.

"Do ya'know what a diamond looks like? asked Waco.

"I know they are what'cha call, in the rough. Not cut an shinny like ya'see in rings. I wouldn't know a rough diamond if'n I saw one."

"Then there's no need fer us to git out there in that water, is it."

"I reckon not. Jason's gona see ta'our needs anyhow."

"Yeah, you got'ta really good friend there, Pecos."

"Yeah."

Chapter 5

Night had fallen on Diamond City and supper had been served at the wagon encampment. All the farmer families were seated on the ground and ate by lantern light and a roaring bonfire. Ollie and Mrs. Fenton were seated a comfortable distance from the bonfire with their guest, the Reverend Jules Blackburn. "You just plain weren't strong enough with'em last night brother Ollie. If'n you want me to, I'd be pleased to hold a sermon in your behalf tonight. I'll show you how to hold a congregation together."

"Would you brother Jules? Would you tell'em how they should all git back together and git on out ta'California."

"Sure will brother Ollie, I'll tell'em."

Ollie stood and shouted over the encampment.

"Folks!! Our gracious guest. Reverend Jules Blackburn, is go'na read us a sermon right after supper is finished!!"

The womenfolk were very pleased and all the men were disgruntled. The men set their plates down and begin to slip away. When Jules Blackburn stood up to address the camp, there were hardly anyone left except the women and children.

"Ladies, as your good Reverend Fenton has done told you. I was intendin' on bringin the word of the Lord to you tonight, but seein' as how them that are needin it worst are not with us. I believe the fittin' thing to do is what the Lord his self would do—that bein as the good book says—to go out and preach the gospel where it's needed most—so, if them hell bent sinners wont come to me.—I reckon I'll have to go to them." Blackburn, in a state of perplexed frenzy, got up and started to leave the encampment and was confronted by Will and Ollie in an attempt to calm him down. Will held on to his arm and tried to hold him back.

"What'cha fixin to do, Jules?"

Jules, infuriated, tried to keep going. He dragged Will along with Will hanging to his arm. Ollie danced around excitedly and kept up with them.

"Like I said. I'm go'na take the word of the Lord to the sinners!!"

"Brother Jules." Ollie said. "That ain't no fittin place to be reading scriptures."

"Fittin' or not they got to be told of their sinnin' ways." Blackburn pulled away from Will and hurried toward his tent up the slope behind Wes's store.

"Tell the farmers bout all the good land out there in California!!" Will called out to Jules.

"They   probably won't even listen to'em, Will."

"Maybe not, Ollie, but if'n he saves one farmer it'll be worth it."

"A-Men!"

The saloon had began to get rowdy and noisey as the men drank and danced with the saloon girls to the loud honkytonk piano. At the end of the bar, Lil bought diamonds and Jason played faro with some customers. Pecos and Waco sat at the bar and drank as they scrutinized Lil's action.

Blackburn entered the saloon carrying a double barrel shotgun. As he made his way through the crowd, he picked up a bottle from a table and took a big drink. He then sit the bottle on the piano top, lifted his foot and shoved the piano player off his stool. He stepped up on the stool, raised the shotgun, pointed up with the butt rested on his hip and addressed the crowd in a very loud voice. A hush fell over the saloon.

"Sinners!!! All you sinners in this den of iniquity! Listen to me!"

"Get down from there! Let's have some music!" A man yelled. Blackburn, without moving the gun butt from his hip, shot off one barrel through the tent top. He leveled the shotgun toward the man and spoke very firm and distinctly. "Let me say first of all. Being as how all your souls are destined to burn in the ever lastin fires of hell. I'll be obliged to send the first one of you what moves to open his mouth for anything other than to take a drink,—on along to his destiny right now."

A dead stillness fell over the room.

"Now let me introduce myself. I'm the Reverend Jules Blackburn, called by the Lord."

Jules took the bottle from the piano top, took a big drink and replaced the bottle as he kept his eyes on the crowd all the while. "To deliver his message to all the unrighteous sinners of this land, and God knows, I've found me a whole flock of 'em here—just sittin round sinnin and braggin bout your riches—yes, and rejoicein in your braggin—The good book says such rejoicein is evil—you rich wretched people—you evil sinners, weep and cry for the miseries that will come upon you. All your riches are corrupted. The good book says your diamonds are evil and they will be a witness to the Lord against you. You've lived in pleasure and sin on this earth. You've nourished your wicked hearts as in a day of slaughter, ever last one of you are evil and has the heart of a snake. How can you ever expect to escape the damnation of ever lastin hell. Woe unto you—you hypocrites. You'll receive the greatest damnation of all. You'll be cast into the lake of fire. That great lake of fire—burning with brimstone."

Pecos and Waco had drink steadily. Waco seemed to enjoy the sermon and Pecos had gone to sleep on the counter with his head on his arms.

Jason looked at Lil bewilderedly and Lil looked at Jason in disgust. Jules took another drink.

"The Lord is known by the judgments what he executes. The wicked is caught up in the works of his own evil hands."

"Hallelujah brother!" Waco shouted. "Hallelujah!"

"If'n it wern't for the two or three good people here in this valley, the good Lord would have done gone an rained down fire and brimstone from heaven and killed the whole damn bunch of you miserable sinners." He reached for the bottle and took another drink.

"Oh yes, hell and destruction ain't never full, and the evil eyes of sinners, like ya'lls eyes, ain't never satisfied." He took another big drink.

"Hallelujah brother!!" Waco shouted.

Will and Ollie stood by the fire in the wagon encampment. Blackburn could be indistinctly heard in the distance delivering his sermon. The womenfolk had long since gave up and went to their wagons.

"Sure wish we could hear what he's tellin'em." Will said.

"Do you think he might of shot somebody, Will?"

"Naugh, I spect he were just gitin their attention."

"Never thought they'd listen." said Ollie.

"He's been at it a long time. Hope he tells'em bout California."

"Sure never thought they'd listen."

"Do you spoze he's mentioned California?"

"I reckon so Will, they're listenin. Never thought they would.?"

Not knowing what else to say, Will and Ollie, set down by the fire and started poking at the coals as they glanced at one another questioningly and tried to hear what Jules was saying in the saloon.

"Be afflicted you sinners—you hypocrites, an mourn an cry—let all your laughter be turned into cryin—an all your joy into heaviness." He reached for the bottle and took another drink.

"As for myself, I will call upon the Lord." He took another drink. "And the good Lord will save me. Ever morn an ever evein—I will pray an I will cry aloud to the good Lord—an he shall hear my voice."

Everyone in the wagon encampment had retired to bed except Will and Ollie who were still by the burned out fire.

"I'm go'na go to bed, Ollie. Don't seem like he's go'na ever git through preachin."

"Longest sermon I ever heared of. Sure didn't think they'ed listen. Night Will."

Will got up and left as Ollie got a handful of twigs and put them on the coals. He got on his knees and blew on the coals until he got a blaze, then put some firewood on it and sit down. Jules Blackburn could still be heard indistinctly from the saloon.

"...an they will go away into their everlastin punishment—cause whosoever therefore is gon'na be a friend of this wicked world..."

He guzzled down the rest of the bottle. "...is go'na be an enemy of God."

Most of the people were asleep with their heads on the table. Some were slouched back in their chair either asleep are passed out. Waco sat at the bar very alert and attentive to Blackburn's sermon.

"Hallelujah, glory be—brother Jules !!" Waco shouted.

Night faded to dawn on Diamond City and the wagon encampment as pre-sunrise colors appeared on the horizon to the sound of Carrie Summers crowing rooster Blackburn continued. But he preached much slower with a hoarse breaking voice, very weary and very drunk. He had dropped the shotgun but still held on to the empty bottle.

"Submit yourselves—therefore to God— resist the devil—and he will flee from you—draw yourself closer to him—and he will draw hisself closer to you—clean up your evil souls—you sinners—an purify—your—hearts."

Blackburn passed out and toppled off the piano stool.

"Hallelujah!" shouted Waco.

Ollie Fenton and Dallas Warbuck sat by the small fire with a coffee pot on it. They had their coat collers turned up to keep the moning dew off their necks and were drinking coffee from tin cups. Will came from around the Summers wagon, dabbled his fingers in a pan of water, splashed some water on his face and walked over to the fire.

"Coffee sure smells good, Ollie." he said as he sit down. He picked up a cup, reached over and poured himself some coffee while he cautiously glanced at Warbuck.

"Ol Jules sure gave'em what fer over at the saloon last night."

He threw Warbuck another quick glance.

"Thought he'd never run down."

Ollie motioned toward Warbuck.

"This here's Dallas Warbuck. He just rode in a while ago."

"Dallas huh? Reckon you must be from Texas?"

"Could be." He said as he poured himself more coffee.

"Name's Will Summers." He extended his hand. Warbuck reluctantly shook his hand. He had developed a habit of being cautious of strangers. In his profession he had to be. His life was always in jeopardy.

"I was kind'a in charge of this here wagon train a'goin to California fore they all got this here diamond fever."

"Done told'em all bout it, Will." said Ollie.

"You got the diamond fever, Mister Warbuck?"

"Not exactly."

"By golly, sure is good to see somebody else what's not got it."

"My Carrie will be fixin vittles in awhile. I'd be pleased if'n you'd join us."

"Well, I—" Warbuck hesitated as he saw Helen emerge from the back of the wagon and begin to wash her face.

"I am sort of hungry, thank'ya kindly Will. I'd be obliged to." he said, as he watched Helen wash and dry her face. He had not seen a woman for a long time. And to see one that looked like an angel destroyed his cautious demeanor and made his insides flutter nervously. He could not keep his eyes off her as she came over and poured herself a cup of coffee. She smiled cheerfully at him.

Chapter 6

Jules Blackburn's congregation from last nights sermon came out of the saloon mumbling, mostly incoherent, about the ordeal they had suffered. Waco came out behind a group of men and called out to them as they staggered off down the street.

"Ya'll sinners better pay heed to the word of the Lord now. Ya'hear !!!"

He looked apprehensively toward the sky as if expecting something.

Warbuck and the entire Summers family were having breakfast.

"You sure fix a fine meal, Mrs. Summers. Can't remember ever having better, or tastier." Dallas said complimentarily.

"Why thank'ya."

Seeing that they had company for breakfast, Carrie had used the eight eggs she saved up from the two a day she got from her two hens and scrambled them with dried beef, and made pan bread, corn meal gruel and graham flour gravy.

"Dallas, what brings'ya here?" Will asked.

All were eating as they talked. Warbuck and Helen were exchanging smiles.

"Everbody's either after diamonds or—"

Carrie interrupted Will.

"More coffee Mister Warbuck?"

Warbuck nodded and Helen jumped up to pour him some coffee as Will continued.

"—or on their way to California."

Helen finished pouring the coffee. She and Dallas were obviously observing one another enamorously.

"Thank'ya, Miss Helen." Dallas said pleasantly.

"Everbody here is either after diamonds or going to California."

"Don't know when I've ate tastier food Mrs. Carrie."

"You're not after diamonds, must be something mighty important. You wouldn't just happen to be goin'ta California, would'ya ?"

"Wha? —oh—no—no, Will. I been trailin a couple of jaspers what's wanted by the law."

"You a lawman, Mister Warbuck ?" Clay asked excitedly.

"Well, sor'ta." Dallas answered reluctantly.

"Helen go fetch water from the creek fer'th washin up." Carrie said.

Helen got a bucket from the wagon and started toward the creek.

"Hold up, Miss Helen, let me help you with the water."

Warbuck caught up with Helen and took the bucket.

"Will them two's gittin friendly alful fast."

"She's a grown girl Carrie. Anyway, it may be good fer him to stay around awhile, what with the talk I've heard of thieving. Him bein a lawman an all."

"Yeah, an I better be a'gittin to my diggins too." Clay said. "They say there's been some claim jumpin further down the creek."

Warbuck stooped down to fill the water bucket.

"Mister Warbuck—Dallas. What will you do when you find the men you're after?—will you?—I mean you want? You seem to be such a kind man. Not the kind of person what would—well—kill somebody. "

"I—I—" Dallas stammered.

"What I mean is, you seem like the kind of man—well—what should have a little farm an be raisin a family."

"I spoze I would'of been by now, if I'd ever met up with the right girl." He stood up and faced Helen.

"I've sure nuff thought along them lines."

"They say there's lots of good farmin land in California."

"Yeah, that's what they say."

"You ain't never killed nobody—have you?"

Dallas ignored her and picked up the bucket of water.

"My husband, Jess.—Storey's daddy." she said reminiscently.

"He was killed by a drunk cowboy, and he never even owned a gun. I don't think I could ever like a man what would shoot another man."

"Did you ever think that if he wore a gun he could have protected himself?"

Helen stared at Warbuck as if in a trance.

"I'm sorry." he said awkwardly. "Bout your husband. I—I—spoze we better get back with the water."

"Ruth, go tell your sister to git on back here with that water."

"Aw shucks, Carrie, leave'em alone. He's the first man she's looked at since Jess got killed."

Dallas and Helen leisurely walked up to the wagon. Dallas sat the bucket down.

"Will" Dallas said. "I think I'll look around some. Where's your boy Clay's diggins at?"

"Down stream a'way."

"Thank's for the meal."

"Might as well have supper with us."

"Thank'ya kindly Will, I'd be mighty pleased. Bye Helen, see'ya later."

Dallas left with a heaviness on his mind that perturbed him greatly. He had just met a woman that could easily be the woman he had laid awake so many nights thinking about. He had told Helen the truth when he said he had thought about settling down. Hadn't a night gone by in the past four or five years that he hadn't laid awake and thought about it. He dreamed of the pleasures he remembered on the farm when he was a young man.

Now this beautiful woman had come into his life and put a swarm of butterflies in his stomach and made his mind mushy. The only thought which he could muster was how to contrariwise her attitude on a man killing criminals or using a gun for self protection.

He knew he certainly wanted to get to know her better and see where it might go from there. "*My God,*" he thought, "*I've only dipped a bucket of water with her and I've never felt like this.*"

He walked down the creek looking like a rough and tough gunslinger who could never have a soft or tender thought in his head, yet feeling like a lovesick puppy. He daydreamed about plowing his crop and Helen walking out into the field in all her splender and beauty, wearing a calico dress and blue sunbonnet, bringing him a jar of cold water. And sitting on the front porch in the evening breeze with her in his lap. His mind raced from one beautiful daydream to another until he reached Clay's claim.

He knew he had never let his mind drift like that when he was in public. It was a dangerous thing to do and it worried him. He conceded that it was a mistake and vowed to never do it again. "*It's a good way to git myself killed.*" he thought.

He briefly remembered a similar situation that occurred out in Tombstone. He had partnered for a short time with a Marshall turned bounty hunter. Together they had brought in a whole family of notorious outlaws. A man and five sons. He and the ex-Marshall had became good friends. But his friend had a problem of letting his mind drift, and it got him killed. The woman that he was infatuated with was a married woman and really not that pretty. Nothing to even compare with Helen. Warbuck knew his friend was mooning over the woman when he was gunned down. That's when he had made it a number one rule in his life, never to daydream. To keep his mind clear, sharp, alert and always on the immediate present moment. And now he was breaking his rule. *"Yes, it's a good way to git myself killed."* he thought.

Warbuck never even contemplated revenge for the death of his friend. He knew the man was not a criminal. He was a jealous husband seeking satisfaction for an injustice. He remembered being exonerated by the Judge in Atlanta when he killed eight men under duress of an injustice. He felt as the Judge did then. It was justifiable homicide.

Warbuck mourned his friends death and saw to it that he had a proper burial before leaving Tombstone.

Clay was in the edge of the creek digging gravel from the bank into a bucket and pouring it into his crudely made rocker to break up the clods and wash the gravel clean. Storey, crouched a little ways from the creek, shot a small stone at Clay with his pea-shooter.

"Storey, if you don't stop that I'm gon'na drag you out here and drown you!"

Dallas Warbuck walked up and stopped by Storey. Storey reached into his overall pocket and took out another small stone and shot it at Clay. The stone hit Clay on the neck. He flinched and ignored it.

"Hey there, Dallas! Thought you'd be lookin fer yer outlaws."

"If'n they're round here. I'll run on to'em soon enough."

"What do they look like, Dallas? Do'ya know'em?"

"Couple of real mean lookin cusses. One ridin a roan. The other a buckskin. They should'of been bout one day ahead of me." He had never seen them up close. But figured that general description would suffice.

Clay excitedly stopped working and waded out of the creek.

"Hey, that must'of been them! Yeah, by golly, it must'of been. It had to be!"

"Had to be what, Clay?"

"Them two what was talkin to Jules yesterday morning. They rode in here an…"

"An what Clay? Where did they go?"

"Well, last I seen of'em after they went to town. They come back by here ridin down the creek with shovels an pans. I reckon to work a spot."

"Uh huh, thank'ya Clay, I spoze they'll be round for awhile. Think I'll mosey back toward town."

Clay waded back into the creek and resumed his work. Storey shot another stone at Clay and ran away laughing.

Warbuck came out of the blacksmith shop and livery stable where he had stopped to check on his horse. He met Waco face to face in the middle of Main street. Both became instantly immobilized in their tracks and stared at each other. They squared off for a showdown. Waco, immediately became very nervous and held his hands out away from his gun.

Warbuck, seeing past Waco, spotted Helen up the street coming toward them.

"Hold on now Mister." Waco pleaded. "Don't go doin nothin hasty. We can talk us a deal. I can pay you more'n you'll git for killin me. Anyway I done changed my ways. I done saw'th light. I done went and got religion.—You wouldn't kill a Christian—would'ya?"

"Where's your partner?" Warbuck asked as his vision slightly shifted to Helen sauntering down the street toward them. His interest was not in Waco's answer. His mind was jumbled and raced a mile a minute as he watched Helen.

"He's round someplace. Me and him's diggin fer diamonds. We can pay'ya more'n we both worth. There's lots of diamond's here. You could even work a spot. You can get rich here. Think of that Mister Warbuck. Think of what's here cept'in a little bounty."

Dallas Warbuck was thinking alright. But not about Waco. His thoughts were on the consequential effect of Helen seeing him kill someone. A look of bewildered anxiety came across his sweaty face. What would be her reaction to seeing him kill this outlaw. He wondered. He swiftly drew his six-shooter and fired three shots in rapid succession knocking Waco back about five feet with each shot, where he fell dead. Warbuck stood in his tracks and witnessed Helen as she became hysterical. She began to scream over and over and show an unnatural lack of self control. She ran her hands through her hair and screamed uncontrollably as she fell to the ground and rolled in the dirt. Warbucks knowing expression changed from that of apprehension to grim reality.

"Yeah." Warbuck said. "I been thinking. Alright, you go on your way for now. We'll talk later."

Helen, unaware of the circumstance, strolled nonchalantly up to Warbuck as Waco hurried away toward the saloon.

"Who was that man." Helen asked.

"Nobody important. Just a drifter."

They walked away arm in arm back down the creek.

Waco went into the saloon and joined Jason and Pecos at a table.

"Pecos, I thought your friend here was go'na take care of Warbuck."

"Don't get jumpy." Jason said. "I will when he gets here."

"Well, he's here!" Waco exclaimed.

Pecos jumped up. Jason looked worried. Waco leaned back in his chair and acted cocky.

"Settle down boys, everthing's okay. I done been talkin ta'em. I talked'em in ta'gittin some diamond's stead of killin us. He ain't so tough after all."

Pecos looked at Waco with astonishment as a smile of relief came over Jason's face.

"But I told'em we'd pay the bounty he's after. So you see'em Jason like you said'ya would, an give'em the—thousand—" He looked at Pecos.

"Yeah Jason, You give'em the thousand dollars."

"Yeah." Waco said. "It's a thousand dollars, Jason. You give it to'em."

Jason's smile faded back to worry. Pecos continued to look at Waco with astonished admiration.

"Yeah, yeah, I'll talk to him." said Jason.

"Ya'better do more'in just talk." Pecos said sternly.

"You really talked to'em didn't you Waco." Pecos exulted "I mean right face to face, you talked to'em." He looked at Jason. "You pay'em real soon, Jason, don't fool round bout it." He turned back to Waco. "You actually really close up talked to'em."

Pecos continued to look at Waco with admiration as Waco leaned back feeling proud of himself. Jason looked at both of them with disgust.

"You boys better get back down to your camp. And stay there until I come down to see you."

Pecos and Waco left as Lil came in.

"Jason, I want to talk to you."

"What have I done now?" He asked puzzled.

"It's about what happened here last night with that preacher." she said as she sat down at the table with him. "On account of him, we hardly bought any diamonds at all, and you. You just stood there and listened to him like everybody else."

"But Lil, I—I—he had a—."

"I don't want to hear any excuses." she interrupted. "This is not a church, or didn't you know that? You just see that nothing like that ever happens again, and there's something else bothering me too. I've heard talk of diamonds being stolen from camps along the creek. Even talk of claim jumpers down stream. Jason, I don't care how much thieving goes on along the creek as long as the diamonds are sold to me, at my price. You see to it word gets out to your two shiftless friends. And while you're at it. Let them know that the Summers boy is said to have the richest diggins on the creek, and he's keeping all of his diamonds. I don't like that Jason, I don't like that at all." She got up to leave and looked back at Jason. "I don't know how I ever got mixed up with scum like you, and them two thieves."

Carrie sat by the wagon mending clothes as she talked to Ruth.

"Ruth, you just don't understan them kind of folks."

"But Maw, they'd pay me good, an the work would be easy. Besides I'd have lots of fun."

"Now Ruth! You're not goin near that saloon, an that's final!"

Will and Storey came around the wagon.

"Good Lord, are you two still squabbling? I'm goin to see how Clay is,   I hear there's trouble further down the creek." As Will and Storey started to walk away. Ollie came up.

"Where ya'been Ollie?"

"Out visitin some of the camps spreadin the word of the Lord."

"Lord knows, these people need it Ollie."

"A-Men."

Will and Storey walked down the creek toward Clay's claim.

"What'cha go'na do Pa'Paw? Ya'gona dig fer diamonds?

"Naugh, Storey. I'm tryin' ta'find a way ta'git us movin' on ta'California.

Diggin' fer diamonds ain't fer us, we're farmers."

"A-Men." said Story.

Will couldn't help a slight unnoticed grin as they continued on to Clays claim.

Chapter 7

Clay was hard at work as he shoveled gravel into his homemade washer. Two typical "backwoods" criminals moved cautiously down a washout toward him. Clay was startled when one of the men spoke.

"You must be the boy we heared tell was doin so good down here."

Clay looked at them but kept working and didn't say anything.

"We kind'a figured maybe you'd let us work this here hole fer'a few days."

Clay still didn't say anything and kept on working.

"I reckon you don't hear too well boy. We're takin over fer'ya, you can rest yerself up fer a spell."

The other man waded out into the water and reached into Clays washer., Clay hit out at him with his shovel.

"Git away from there! Git away!"

Clay drew back the shovel and swung it again, knocking one of the men down in the water. The other man waded out into the water, grabbed the shovel and pulled Clay down. Clay got up yelling and swinging wildly at the man as the other man got up and both tried to subdue Clay. He knocked one of them over the gravel washer. The other one grabbed him from behind in a bear hug. Clay was yelling and trying to get loose. Will came running up the creek bank with Storey right behind him. He didn't stop when he reached them but dove straight away onto the back of the man holding Clay. They all went down into the water. As they all three were getting up, Will knocked the other man down with a haymaker and waded over to see about Clay. Clay was getting up slowly as the two men slipped and stumbled up the bank and ran up the washout to where they left their horses. Will helped Clay out of the creek onto the bank. Storey jumped up and down yelling and throwing clods across the creek toward the claim jumpers as they ran away.

Will and Clay had gotten out of the creek and were sitting on the bank. A small crowd had gathered to see what the commotion was. Dallas and Helen approached through the crowd and stooped down by Will and Clay.

"What happened Will? Are ya'll okay?" asked Dallas.

Will, to exhausted to talk, looked at him and grinned.

"Couple of men tried'ta push me out'ta my diggins, but me an Paw, we showed'em!"

Storey tugged at Warbuck, telling him to go after them and pointed out across the creek. Helen pulled Storey away to calm him down.

The other miners started breaking up and going back up and down the creek. Two or three miners were left as Will and Warbuck stood up.

"Must'of been them claim jumpers I've been hearin bout from down the creek." said Will.

"Sure better start watchin our goods." A miner said. "Some of my diamonds done come up missin from my tent. Had'em hid real good to, only'est me and the madam knowed where they'us hid."

Pecos and Waco walked up going toward town. They stopped to see what was going on. Dallas saw them and moved out to the side away from everyone else and without taking his eyes off of them he spoke to Will.

"Will, you and Clay go on to the wagon and get out of those wet clothes."

Out of habit, Warbucks gun hand hang loosely to his side and his fingers twitched. Pecos and Waco saw his cold stare and cautiously began to back away. Helen too, could not help but to see the firmness in his face and the deadly look in his eyes, and his gun hand become ridged in the drawing position just inches from his gun. It frightened her immensely but she held her fear and acted unaware of the tense situation. Holding Storey by the hand she courageously stepped directly between Dallas and the outlaws and spoke to Will.

"Come on Paw, me an Storey will walk back to the wagon with'ya!"

Pecos and Waco, as Helen had suspected, took advantage of the situation and hurriedly departed toward town.

Jason Ransom stood in front of the saloon talking with some miners when he spotted Pecos and Waco coming toward him. He stepped out into the street and met them.

"Glad you boys are here. Let's walk on up the way where we can talk."

Jason glanced back toward the saloon as they walked up the street through the commotion of other people and wagons. He was checking to be sure that Lil had not come out and watched him.

"Jason, you got'ta go pay Warbuck." said Waco.

"I'll take care of it, but right now we've got to have a talk."

They left the street and went up the slope a short way where they sat on the ground.

"What'cha got on yer mind, Jason?" asked Pecos.

"You boys would like to get rich, wouldn't you? Well, it's time you went to work. This is the best opportunity you'll ever have, and you only have to get rid of one person."

"Now hold on Jason." Waco said. "You said no killin an I sure ain't killin no woman!"

"This is only an old farmer. No one will even miss him."

"Then why git rid of him. What good would it do?"

"He has a boy that's sitting right on top of the best pocket on this creek. Now, the boy will be easy. What's in our way is the old man." Jason continued as an afterthought, more to himself. "*Besides, he has something else I want.*"

"What about the plan to take over Lil's place an git her diamonds?"

"That will come later. First I want Will Summers out of the way. And I want his boys claim."

"Will Summers? That's the old man the claim jumpers just tried to take!" Pecos exclaimed.

"Yeah, and he's a friend of Warbucks." said Waco.

"What about Warbuck?" Pecos asked. "You got'ta do what you said bout him. We go an kill a friend of his, then just what do'ya think Warbuck's go'na do?"

"I ain't goin against that bounty hunter. Ain't no way." said Waco.

"Tell'ya what Jason." Pecos said. "You do what'ya said. You buy off Warbuck. An then when he's long gone from here. We do your work. Fer half the diamonds."

"Half the diamonds! You two should have plenty of diamonds, with all the stealing that's been going on from the tents up and down the creek."

"We ain't the ones." Pecos said. "We ain't stole nothing."

"Yeah." Waco said. "What'da'ya think we are, anyway."

"I don't know what you are Waco, but I know Pecos. He would kill his grandma if the price was right. I figured since you was riding with him, that you're probably no better than he is."

Pecos and Waco were astounded by the angry outburst from Jason. "I thought you boys wanted to get rich, but I guess I was wrong."

"Pecos" Waco asked. "Would you really kill you're grandma?"

"I don't care what they said." Pecos was furious. "She died of natural causes."

That curve struck both Waco and Jason dumbfounded.

"Alright boys," Jason said. "We're bickering like school kids. *"That grandma bit"* he thought. *"Really struck a nerve. I guess it hit to close to home. I'd better try to appease him."* Let's pull this job off and you'll get your half of the boys diamonds. You know I'll be fair with you. No reason we can't all be rich. *"Half for y'all, half for Lil and half for me.yeah, sure."* he thought.

Waco still wondered about Pecoses grandmother.

Jason got up and left, telling them he would be back later and they could make plans how to do it. Waco watched him leave and looked questioningly at Pecos. "Who said ya'killed yer grandma?"

Pecos rolled with laughter. "If'n I ever even had a grandma" he said. "I never knew it." he continued to laugh as he pointed his finger at a befuddled Waco and said. "Had'ya goin, didn't

I partner." and continued to laugh. Waco, in a delusional state of confusion, reluctantly joined him in laughter.

Carrie had a bowl over Storey's head giving him a haircut when Will came out the back of the wagon. He had changed his shirt and overalls and he sit his brogans on the tailgate in the sunshine to dry.

"Carrie, where's Helen an Dallas?"

"They went walkin off over'th hill yonder, up to the pine trees. I ain't so sure I like it none either, Will."

"Well at least she ain't bawlin."

"A-Men." said Storey.

Will and Carrie both gave Storey an admonishing look as Ollie walked up with bible in hand.

"I was just thinkin Will. Ya'll have a lot'ta diamonds from Clay's diggins. couldn't we just hire another guide to lead us on to California?"

"You've visited an talked to bout everbody along this creek, Ollie. Do'ya know anybody what knows the way?"

"No, I reckon not."

"Maybe you ought'ta try fer some diamonds, so's ta help build your church once we do git'ta California."

"The Lord provides what I need, Will."

Chapter 8

Scattered streams of bright sunshine shown through the tall majestic pine. Dallas and Helen walked hand in hand through the soft pine straw. He held on to her hand as if he thought she may get away while he tried to think of how to tell her that he had killed many men. Telling her he only killed men that needed killing, he didn't think would work. Helen's mind was wandering elsewhere. His big strong hand squeezing her hand stimulated her. She wondered if that hand could drive a woman mindless with pleasure. Dallas was taken with Helen as well and his thoughts were suddenly about how it might feel to have her in his arms and explore her curvaceous body. He unknowingly squeezed her hand tighter.

"Dallas, you're hurting my hand!"

"Oh, I'm sorry, I didn't realize." He lifted her hand, massaged it and kissed it tenderly. "Helen?" he looked deeply into her eyes. "Why did you step between me and the outlaws? I know you did it on purpose. What was you thinking?"

Helen backed away and stared at him. She thought she had pulled a fast one. She walked around wondering how to answer him. She felt his gaze locked on her, but pretended not to notice. After a time, she turned and faced him. "Paw told me how men try to kill famous gunmen to build a reputation. He said if you didn't have a gun to protect yourself you would of done been killed. Like Jess was. Do you ever get tired of being provoked into gunfights? Tired of killing men who want to prove that they're faster with a gun than you."

Taking his eyes from her for the first time since they stopped. Dallas removed his hat and tossed it on the ground.

"A man in my position. With my reputation. Can't afford to turn his back on a challenge and walk away without being called a coward or getting shot in the back." He grinned slightly and chuckled. "I see, so you took that chance believing you were helping me. I earned my reputation by defending myself, not by looking for trouble."

"No, I just didn't want you to kill them in front of Storey, and me."

Dallas moved over closer to her and met her challenging gaze. He took her into his arms and kissed her passionately, taking full control of her senses. When he released her. He walked away going back down the slope.

Helen stared at his back as she stroked her tingling lips and inhaled deeply to slow her racing heart. She picked up Dallas's hat and started down the slope after him. Within only a minute or two she had caught up to him. She knew he had purposely walked slow. She put her arm around him and walked a short distance into an area covered with wild flowers. Without saying anything, she pulled him down into a sitting position. He laid back on the ground and pulled her down beside him. She laid her head on his chest.

"Ya'know Helen, I been doing a lot of remembering and a lot of thinking. My parents were farmers. My Paw taught me a lot about farming. I really liked it. I miss them and the farm but I try not to think about it. Ya'know, I done told you before that I've thought about gettin a little farm and settlin down if I ever found the right woman to settle with.

Helen raised her head and looked wide eyed into Dallas's eyes.

"Dallas, what're you trying to say?"

"I'm tryin to ask you if'n you'll settle down an farm with me."

"Dallas, don't be teasin with me."

"I'm not teasin. I mean it.—I—I love you."

He put his hand behind her head and pulled her down slowly until their lips met. He kissed her with tender affection.

"I know you don't rightly take to killing, so I'm going to make you a promise. I'll not be doing any killing unless it's to protect you and Storey."

"What about Clay and Ruth?"

"Okay, them too."

"And Maw and Paw?"

"Yeah, them too."

"And yerself? Ya' got to protect yerself."

"Yeah, okay."

Will sat on the tailgate of the wagon putting on his brogans.

"Carrie," he said. "I'm goin back down and talk to Clay bout us tryin'ta make it by ourselves." He got down and headed for the creek.

Jules Blackburn, on the ground by the creek, was leaned on his elbow hiccupping.

"Mornin brother Jules" Will said. "Are ya'go'na hold another sermon at the saloon tonight?"

"I don't reckon God hisself could save that bunch, brother Will."

"Yeah, I spoze it would take a miracle alright."

Will resumed his walk down the creek. He saw Reverend Ollie Fenton across the creek in front of a miners tent reading from his bible to a group of miners womenfolk.

Little Storey concentrated on a large pot of boiling beans as his grand-mother stirred them and poked the fire. Dallas and Helen entered the campsite from the backside and came around the wagon.

"Howdy Mrs. Carrie. Sure does smell good."

He mussed Storey's hair and kept walking toward the creek.

"Where you two been, Helen?" asked Carrie.

"Just out walkin, Maw."

"Helen, you two are gittin a mite friendly. You know how you feel bout guns and men what kill people."

"But Maw, people have to protect their selves"

"I'm beginnin to feel like you, Helen. I'm just a bout wishin we'd stayed back home."

"Why, Maw." Helen said, somewhat melodramatic. "You know there's nothin back there. Just think how much better things are gona be out in California."

Carrie dropped her stirrer in the pot and looked at Helen with absolute amazement. Storey took a small stone from his pocket and dropped it into the bean pot. He watched it inquisitively and then did it again.

A group of miners had gathered in the street in front of the saloon. They were angry and wanted something done about the stealing that had been going on.

"Here comes Warbuck." Jake said. "Let's talk to him bout it."

"Alright Jake, you talk to'em." A miner said. There were a few voices of approval and they all got quiet as Warbuck reached them.

"Mister Warbuck, sir" Jake said. "You bein a lawman and such—we kind'a figured you might would help us."

"What's the trouble?" he asked prowdly with an inflated ego for being called a lawman.

"It seems that everbody here has been comin up with diamonds missin from their stashes. —Whoever is takin'em don't never take'em all— just a few each time. —Some of the men has got it in their heads that Lil is behind it all, an they're want'in to run her out."

"Is there any proof that it's Lil?"

"Naw, ain't none, but that ain't stopping them. I figered if'n you would look into it. Maybe ya' could find out fer sure who it is."

"Alright men. Ya'll break it up an go on bout yer work. I'll see what I can find out."

The miners were quiet for awhile and looked around at each other.

"Might as well let'em try." someone in the crowd said.

There were reluctant sounds of approval as the crowd dispersed and Warbuck headed into the saloon.

"Thank's Mister Warbuck!" said Jake.

Warbuck wondered, only briefly, why men that was his elder always called him mister. Lil sat behind the bar examining some diamonds. A shotgun was on the bar beside her and a couple of saloon girls were straightening tables. Warbuck stopped at the bar in front of her.

"I want to thank you for what you done out there." Lil said.

"Least I could do under the circumstances. You know anything bout what they're sayin?"

"Nothing for sure. But I've got my suspisions."

"Suspicions?" "What kind?"

"Well, there's these two no account drifters hanging around with my gambler, Jason Ransom. Now, Jason's about as rotton as they come, but these two. They've got to have him beat all to pieces."

"I know of them two. What makes you think it's them?"

"Like I said. Just my suspisions."

Lil poured a drink and pushed it across the bar to Starbuck.

"I understand that you're a friend of the Summers family."

He took the drink and downed it.

"I've been eatin with'em."

A word of advise. Watch the young girl. Jason's got eyes for her. And like I said. He's rotten."

Warbuck started to pay for the drink.

"No, it's on the house." she said.

"Thanks."

Warbuck went out the door. Lil put the tray of diamonds in her safe and locked it.

Helen dished up a plate of beans for Warbuck as he entered the camp. They both sat down and started to eat.

"Where's Ruth?" Warbuck asked.

"She's over helping Mrs. Fenton." Carrie answered.

"Where's Will?"

"He's at the diggins with Clay."

Warbuck took a bite of beans and began to chew. He chewed about three times and grimaced in pain. He took a small stone from his mouth and threw it away. He sat his plate down and got up. Helen also got up.

"You want to go walkin, Dallas?" she asked.

"Later Helen, right now I've got to go talk to Will."

Clay sat on the bank and Will was propped up on one elbow.

"But Paw, how can'ya think'a bout goin off an leavin all these diamonds here in'th creek."

"What good are they go'na do'ya boy? You can't plant'em an watch'em grow."

"It's money Paw, it's wealth, we can buy anything we want."

"Anything we want! What'da'ya want Clay? Somthin ya'don't need? You want'ta buy yer vittles out'ta a store? Look here, Clay." Will sat up and picked up a hand full of dirt. He held it out toward Clay and let it sift through his fingers. "This is what a man needs son. The good earth. This is what grows yer vittles. Not a bunch of pretty stones. Not money. This is real God given wealth!"

"Been lookin fer'ya Will." Dallas said as he walked up to them. "How's the diggin comin along Clay?"

"Hi, Dallas, okay I spoze."

"I been tryin to talk some sense in'ta Clay." Will said. "It's time we was movin on. Guide or no guide."

"Be a rough trip without a trail guide." Warbuck said. "Helen and Mrs. Carrie has bout got supper ready. Why don't ya'll go eat."

"I'm not hungry." Clay said.

"Might as well." Will said. "Ain't doin no good here."

"I'm go'na stay here awhile." Dallas said. "Tell Helen I'll be there at supper, and Will. Kind'a keep an eye on Ruth."

Will hesitated and looked questioningly at Dallas. He then turned and walked away.

Dallas sat on the bank and watched Clay wade into the creek and go to work washing gravel.

"You seen anything else of them two what I was trailin."

"They come back and forth a lot. When'ya go'na git'em?"

"Hadn't had time yet." Dallas said.

"Yeah, Ruth sez'ya been spinnin all you're time sparkin Helen."

"Uh-huh."

Ollie Fenton stood in front of a tent back from the creek with his open bible in his hand. The womenfolk which he had been reading scriptures to were gathered around him. One lady came out of the tent. Ollie took off his hat and placed it upside down on his bible.

"—and now ladies, ya'll may make your love offerin for the Lord's work in the usual manner. And remember that them who gives shall also receive."

The women went by Ollie in single file and dropped two or three diamonds each into his hat. Ollie acknowledged each contributor with "God bless you sister."

Leaned against a cottonwood tree near the walk bridge, Ruth Summers looked across the creek at the excitement along Main street. She watched Wes taking inventory in front of the mercantile store. With a pad and pencil he counted shovels in a barrel. Ruth counted with him as he moved them from one side of the barrel to the other. She counted twenty shovels and then a saloon girl caught her eye as she came out of the tent and threw out a pan of water into the street. Her heart skipped a beat as Jason Ransom came out of the saloon. He saw her right away and knew without a doubt that she stood over there waiting to see him. He smiled real big and threw her a kiss. She smiled enticingly and returned the kiss just as Lil walked out and saw them.

Mrs. Fenton sat on a cane bottom chair beside the Fenton wagon, sewing, as Ollie walked up.

"Where'ya been Ollie?"

"Out workin fer the Lord."

"You're a good man, Ollie. Not like that Reverend Blackburn."

"Jules is'a good man, he means well, just don't go bout it right, that's all."

"The Lord prospers them what obeys him." Mrs. Fenton said.

"A-Men."

Ollie climbed up into his wagon.

Dallas Warbuck stood up and stretched his legs.

"Be night soon Clay. What say we go on to the wagon?"

"I'll be stayin here, least I find my diggins full of claim jumpers come mornin."

"I'll fetch'ya something to eat. I've got'a go see bout my hoss."

"An Helen?"

"Yeah." Dallas said as he walked away and hurried to the wagon.

Helen stood at the back of the wagon waiting anxiously for Dallas. "We still got time to go walkin, If'n we hurry." she said.

Dallas took her by the hand and they walked slowly around the wagon until they were out of sight and then broke into a run up the slope and toward the large stand of wildflowers. Once in the wildflowers they fell down laughing and breathing heavily. Intoxicated by the sweet aroma of lilac, lavender, indigo and violet, Dallas leaned toward her and their lips met. He reached out and put his arms around her and pulled her to him.

She came willingly, still locked in his kiss, then wildly they kissed and clung to each other. He felt her body all along the length of his, and he lost his mind to the strong desire of overpowering eroticism. Suddenly, like a flash, a streak of raw nature not to be denied its due, took over. Helen said nothing. Nor did he. They were one body, one will, before even they were joined in love, he stripped away some of their clothing, she took the rest from him and herself. —Helen was limp beneath him when he regained his senses—and his breath. He then realized that she was weeping.

"What is it? What's wrong? Did I hurt you?"

"No, no." she sobbed. "It was wonderful. I'm only cryin from happiness."

Dallas had only known profane love, from brothels and an occasional saloon girl. Now he knew another kind. Simple, pure, impassioned and very, very good.

Chapter 9

From the corner of the mercantile store, the recognizable voice of Dallas Warbuck was heard distinctly by Pecos and Waco as they were about to enter the saloon.

"Pecos!"

They stopped in their tracks as fear gripped them.

"Pecos, I want to talk to you and Waco over here."

They moved cautiously past the café and over to Warbuck.

"I just wanted to tell'ya, long as there ain't no trouble here. I'm forgettin bout the bounty on ya'll."

"Wont be no trouble from us." Pecos said in a relieved tone.

"Wont be none, no sir, we done changed our ways. Did I tell'ya I'm a Christian now. I done went an got religion."

"I'll be watchin ya'll."

Pecos and Waco hurried to the saloon. Warbuck stood by the mercantile store for a little while and then followed them into the saloon. He stopped just inside the door and surveyed the situation before making his way to the bar beside Pecos and Waco. He ordered a drink and turned to look at Jason gambling with a group of men. Jason spotted him staring at him and became extremely frightened. He continued to look sternly at Jason as he downed his drink, placed the glass and money on the bar and walked by Jason and out the door. A look of relief came across Jason's face as he tried to hide his fear. Lil had watched with concern from the end of the bar. She could not control her laughter as she watched Jason try to compose himself.

Clay warmed his hands over a small fire in front of his lean-to. He jumped up startled as Warbuck walked up.

"It's just me Clay, yer Maw sent a plate of vittles. I'm fraid they're cold though. I left'em in front of the store awhile."

"I'll eat'em anyway."

"Kind'da figered'ya would. I got'ta be goin right back. Didn't git a chance'ta see bout my hoss."

Clay looked at him and grinned. He sat down and started to eat as Dallas turned to leave.

"Thank'ya for the vittles."

"Yer welcome."

Dawn had broken and it neared sun-up when Will came out of the wagon encampment taking long strides toward the walk bridge while he fastened up his over-alls. He looked mad enough to kill as he headed behind the saloon and up the slope where there were a line of tents. He knew which one was Jason's. He had seen him go in and out of it on occasion. He went directly to the tent, jerked open the flap and went inside. The world stopped momentarily and then started up with the most excruciating yelling and screaming ever heard. It echoed throughout the valley awakening everyone. The nearest people were running out to see what was happening. The tent shook and trembled as the loud screaming pursued. Will emerged from the tent flap dragging the screaming Jason Ransom by one leg in his long johns.

Jason grabbed the tent and pulled it down as Will pulled him down the slope, by the saloon and into the street. A large crowd had gathered and was watching Will hit him with full swings every time he got part way up. Some of the miners finally pulled Will off of him and held him back as Jason, afraid to get up crawled back up the slope and half way under his fallen tent. Will kicked at him and tried to get loose from the miners. Warbuck arrived on the scene and looked at Will yelling at Jason with his rear in the air sticking out from under the fallen tent.

The miners were still holding Will back.

"If'n I ever see'ya as much as look at'er agin. I'll kill'ya. You worthless scum!"

Warbuck could hardly hold back his laughter.

"What's the matter, Will. What did he do?"

"I finally got it out of'er Dallas, I finally got it out. It took all night, but I finally got it out."

"Got what out, Will?"

"Got it out'ta Ruth. Why I got'ta keep an eye on'er, that's what."

Warbuck took Will by the arm and the other men let him go.

"Come on Will, let's go to the wagon."

Warbuck left with Will, going back across the walk bridge and toward the wagon. He had a tremendous job controlling his laughter. Will looked at him bewilderingly and wondered why he was laughing.

Carrie had put the coffee pot over the fire and gone to the wagon to get a a bread pan. She turned around as Will and Warbuck showed up.

"Coffee will be ready in awhile. You didn't kill'em did'ya Will?"

"Naugh, he'll live."

Will went to the wagon and Warbuck went to the fire. He warmed his hands and then sat down next to the fire, Carrie came over to check the coffee.

"Sounded like quite a ruckus." said Carrie.

"Yes'um, it sure was."

"I was a'feared that was go'na happen. I sure do wish we'd find us a guide. So's we could leave this place."

"Didn't Helen tell'ya last night?" asked Dallas. "I'm go'na guide ya'll on to California."

Carrie stepped back astonished and looked at Warbuck.

"You   go'na   what?   You—well,   I—I never—I—"

She excitedly started hollering for Will.

"Will—Will, come out here! Will, did'ya hear that—Will, come out here Will!!!"

Will, thinking something had happened to Carrie, came out the back of the wagon very fast and excited. He stumbled, fell, and got up yelling.

"What's a matter Carrie?!!   What's a matter?!!"

"Will, did'ya hear that? He's go'na guide us. Dallas is go'na guide us."

"You mean to California?"

"That's what he said. Sittin right there, just now. He said it, didn't'ya Dallas?"

"Dallas? You—I mean—do you—is she foolin? Do you know the way?"

"Been there a couple of times." said Dallas.

Will was wide eyed with his mouth open as he stared at Dallas.

"Now ya'll wait just a minute." Will said. "Don't nobody move. Let me see if'n I heared right."

Will held the same expression and bent over with his hands on his legs above his knees, so as to look directly into Warbucks eyes. He held that position for a few moments without moving. He then suddenly started jumping up and down with jubilation, slapping his legs with his hands and dancing around joyfully, singing incoherently.

Helen came from the Fenton wagon and sat down beside Dallas.

"Ya'll sure makin a lot'a racket this fine morning."

"Thought you was go'na tell'em last night." said Dallas.

"I couldn't, what with Paw and Ruth carryin on like they was."

Carrie went over to the fire, bent down and hugged Helen and Dallas, smiled and wiped her eyes with her apron. Will suddenly became very serious.

"How am I ever go'na get Clay out'ta that creek?"

Ollie Fenton came over to the fire. He stooped down to feel the coffee pot and jerked back his hand. He stuck his finger in his mouth.

"What's a matter, Ollie. The coffee pot hot?" asked Will.

"Nope, it just don't take me long to feel a pot." Ollie quipped. "What's all the excitement bout over here?"

"Ya'll can start gittin ready, Ollie." Will said. "Dallas is go'na guide us to California."

"Praise the Lord."

"Me and Dallas is gitten married up to." Helen revealed happily.

"Glory be ta-bessy, this is some day of surprises." Will exclaimed as he jumped up and shook Dallas's hand.

Carrie hugged Helen and Dallas again and started crying from happiness.

"I'll go git some coffee cups, everybody else is to busy crying." Will said jubilantly. Carrie raised up wiping her face with her apron.

"I'll help'ya Will." she said, as she followed him to the wagon.

"Ya'll let me marry'ya soon as we git to California." said Ollie.

"California nothin." You'll do it soon as we leave this place."

Helen got up and went over to the wagon where Will and Carrie were embraced and crying with joy. She put her arms around them.

"Well, Mister Fenton." Dallas said. "I guess if'n we're go'na have any coffee, we've got to go git us a cup." He started to get up and saw Will coming with the cups.

"Ollie, check the pot an see if'n the coffee is still hot." said Will.

"I'm sure it's plenty hot enough." he replied.

They sat and enjoyed the coffee for awhile before speaking.

"Will," Dallas said. "I guess we better start gittin things ready to go. You talk to the farmers an see if any of them want to come along. We should be leavin a little after daybreak in'a mornin."

He sat his cup down, stood up, turned to leave, then turned back to Will.

"Will, leave Clay'ta' me. I'll figer out somethin."

Jason, fully clothed, had tied a guy rope from the back of his tent to a stake in the ground. He heard Pecos call softly from the path in front of the tent. He walked around to the front looking very haggard and sporting a huge blackened eye.

"What do you two want this early?"

"Hey Jason, what happened to you?" asked Waco. Jason stared at him angrily and didn't answer. Waco, although seeming to be amused by Jasons appearance, saw the seriousness in his angry look and didn't say anything else about it.

"We talked it over last night." Pecos said. "An we figered maybe it would be best if we rode on."

"Yeah." Waco said. "We ain't lookin to go against Warbuck."

"You can't go now." Jason pleaded. "Not now, not when I got this good idea. Listen, carry this out, and you can both leave here rich. You want to get rich. Don't you?"

"We keep hearing bout gittin rich." Pecos said. "But we ain't seen none of it yet."

"Yeah Jason." Waco said. "Show us some rich."

They had been walking while talking and were not aware of where they were. Jason put his hand on Pecoses chest to stop him from walking. They stopped next to a canvas tent.

"At least listen to my plan." Jason said. "See what you think about it."

"Were listenin." Pecos said.

" Alright then. Here's the plan."

Unbeknownst to them, Lil was standing close to the inside wall of the tent listening to them. She moved over closer to the canvas wall to better hear.

"Then after we kidnap the Summers boy. We'll tie him up and hide him out up in the hills and make the old man give us his diamonds to get him back."

"I don't know." Pecos said. "We mess with them Summers and we've got Warbuck on us."

"Yeah." Waco said. "And I don't want none of him."

"You want those diamonds don't you? Listen, they'll never know who done it. Not before we've got the diamonds and long gone."

"I don't know." Pecos said. "It does sound like a good plan."

He looked at Waco for an answer.

"I just don't want to tangle up with that bounty hunter." said Waco.

"We'll think bout it Jason," Pecos said. "You come down to our camp this evein. We'll let you know then."

Pecos and Waco turned and left with Jason still talking.

"Alright, you boys think it over." Jason said. "And while you're at it think of how rich you will be."

Jason turned the other way and directly into the saloon door. As he came into the saloon he was confronted by Lil.

"So you didn't get enough of old man Summers this morning, did you?"

Jason was disoriented and wondering what he was doing in the saloon.

"Wha—what'll you mean?"

"You know darn well what I mean. I heard your plans with those no account trail bums.

Jason felt very disheartened.

"Well for once Jason, you're beginning to use your head."

Jason brightened up and felt pleased with himself.

"Just you don't forget. My cut is still one half."

Jason again felt disheartened.

Pecos and Waco were laid back on their saddles in front of a tree limb lean-to in a clump of trees. Their horses were tied nearby.

"I still think we best go on and ride out." said Waco.

"Yeah, but I sure hate to leave without even one diamond." said Pecos.

"Yeah, me too." Waco said. "But that friend of your'n, he ain't go'na help us git none. I don't trust him, Pecos. He ain't go'na do us no good—none a'tall."

"I been thinkin that too. So I came up with us a plan."

"What kind'a plan, Pecos?"

"We go'na rob ol' Lils safe, an git all those diamonds she's been buyin up, then high tail it out'ta here. An I'm thinkin that our friend Jason is go'na git all the blame. It won't take no work hardly at all. Five or six sticks of dynamite ought'ta pop that little old safe right open. Then we just scoop up them pouches of diamonds—jump on our hosses and ride."

"Tell me again Pecos—a little slower—an what's ol' Lil go'na do ta' Jason?" Waco brightened up at the thought of Lil blaming Jason and he started to laugh. Pecos started laughing with him. Pecos stopped laughing and became serious.

"We'll do it right after daybreak while everbody is still asleep, sept'in Jason—I'm thinkin he'll be out kidnappin."

"Yeah out kidnappin." Waco said. "An ol'Lils go'na git him. She's go'na git him good."

They both started laughing again, enjoying thinking about what Lil was going to do to Jason. Waco began rolling on the ground laughing hysterically.

From the doorway of the saloon Lil called.

"Mister Warbuck!"

Dallas was talking to Wes in front of his store. He looked over toward the saloon and acknowledged Lil. He then walked over to see her.

"Something I want to tell you bout Jason and them two friends of his. They've been makin plans to kidnap the Summers boy to git his diamonds."

"Why are you tellin this to me. Don't he work for you."

"Seems like he's workin more for himself than fer me. Sure I'm here to make money, just like everbody else, but I'll only go so far to do it."

"You know when they're plannin to do it?"

"No, they was talkin bout it this morning. I happened to overhear them."

Lil looked down the street and saw Jason coming toward the saloon.

" Here comes Jason now."

As Jason approached, Warbuck tipped his hat to Lil.

"Yes Mam, sure is a nice day!" He walked away.

Jason looked at him, then at Lil.

"What did he want?"

"Just being neighborly."

Lil went into the saloon. Jason had a very worried feeling and turned to look in the direction which Warbuck left. He watched him greet a couple of miners on their way to the creek and stop at the livery stable.

Carrie and Helen were cheerfully smiling and humming as they went about their cooking chores. Will was currying his team. Ollie and Mrs. Fenton were sitting by their wagon.

"It's sure pleasin news bout us leavin tomorrow." she said.

"A-Men" he said. "Can't hardly wait. The Lord's go'na have the biggest and finest church ever in California.

"You're a good man, Ollie."

"A-Men."

Chapter 10

Jules Blackburn sat on the creek bank and watched Clay work.

"The Lord would surely bless'ya if'n you'd let me work yer diggins fer just a bit."

"I'm bein blessed plenty good already."

"Some of your good fortune should go ta'God."

"You sit foot in my diggins Reverand an you go'na go someplace."

"Now brother Clay, that ain't no way ta'be."

"Hi there, Dallas!" Clay exclaimed as Warbuck walked up behind Blackburn.

Blackburn turned and looked. He jumped up.

"Fine day, ain't it Mister Warbuck.—Well, best I better git to work."

Clay got out of the creek and put the coffee pot on a small fire in front of his lean-to.

"Might as well sit a spell, an let's have some coffee."

Warbuck sat down close to the fire and started poking at the coals with a stick.

"I've got'ta talk ta'ya some Clay."

"Bout what?" He looked at him curiously.

Carrie and Ruth stretched a rope between two trees and were hanging wet clothes out to dry.

"Helen was carry'in on with that Dallas man. Whyn't Paw whoop him?"

"It ain't the same Ruth. Anyway they's go'na git hitched up. Maybe someday you'll understan."

"Maybe me'an Jason could of got hitched up too."

Carrie stopped working and looked at Ruth with an admonishing disgust.

"God forbid, girl, that you ever git married up to any of them kind'a people!"

Clay took a sip of coffee and looked at Warbuck.

"I'm surely pleased bout you an Helen." he said. "But I got the same right'ta change my life as you. An I don't want ta'leave here."

"You know yer Paws go'na be mighty heartbroken.—besides he needs'ya'ta help in gitten settled an all."

"But there's still lot's'a diamonds here!"

"Your folks ought'ta come first Clay, besides— Warbuck cut his eyes to see Clays reaction as he continued in a conducive manner.—there's lots more gold in California than there is diamonds here."

"There is? You sure bout that?"

"Yep, I've been there. I've seen the camps with my own eyes. They been havin big strikes there for some time now. Havin new ones all the time. This here place ain't nothin compared to the gold strikes out there."

"Why didn't'ya tell'me bout the gold a'fore?"

He jumped up excited.

"Let's go!"

"Whoo boy, slow up now, we'll be leavin first thing in'a'mornin."

"You go on in an help yer Paw git ready to go."

"Okay, I'll clean up what's left in the washer an be in bout super time."

"Be sure now. I'd like'ya to stay in the camp tonight."

"I'll be in." he said. "I'm ready'ta git on'ta good ol'California."

Clay waded back into the creek as Warbuck went toward town.

Ollie sat reading his bible as Will approached his wagon.

"Reckon we'll be the only'est ones goin." Will said. "Rest of'em got the fever to bad."

"I'm ready to roll." Ollie said. "Soon's I hook up my team in'a mornin."

"Yer a good man, Ollie."

Ollie was pleased with himself.

Warbuck went toward town and met Jason Ransom going downstream.

"Ransom, when' ya see your two friends, tell'em fer me, to remember what I told'em."

"What's that?"

"They'll understan."

Warbuck proceeded on toward town. Jason, bewildered, proceeded on downstream. He came upon Jules Blackburn sitting on the creek bank with his bottle in his hand.

"You give up preachin, Reverend?"

"Can't save'a soul what's aready willed ta'the devil."

Jason looked intently at Clay washing gravel and picking a diamond from his washer.

"How's luck, young man?"

"Can't complain." said Clay.

"I hear tell you're doing real well. Hope you're keeping your diamonds hid real good."

"Good enough."

"Guess your Paw is keeping them?"

"Could be."

"You take care, now."

Jason left, going on downstream as Clay called out to Blackburn.

Blackburn got up and moved over to Clays claim as Clay got out of the creek and started blowing on the coals to start his fire. Blackburn sat down beside him.

"What'cha want?" asked Blackburn.

"You been itchin' ta'git in'ta my claim. What'cha give me fer it ?"

"You serious boy? You want'in'ta sell?"

"Don't know yet. Make me'a offer."

"I only got four little diamonds. Don't spoze that would be enough?"

"Reverend Jules, ya'know, I been thinking. It's bout time that I done somthin fer'th Lord's work. I think I'm go'na let'ya have this here claim fer yer four diamonds."

Blackburn jumped up and looked inquisitively at Clay a few seconds before replying.

"You really mean it, don't'cha!! Glory hallelujah!"

"Brother Clay, the Lord's go'na surely bless'ya fer this. Let me git my shovel."

"Hold up there, Jules. You just git me your diamonds. Ya'can move in here soon's I leave this eve'nin."

"Alright, Brother Clay. I'll go ta'my tent an git'em. The Lord sure do work in mysterious ways to prosper them what love's him."

Pecos and Waco were laid back on their saddles. Both sat up as Jason walked up and squated down in front of them.

"You boys thought it over?" asked Jason.

"We been thinkin on it real hard." Pecos said. "And the best way we figure it is this. The best time ta'git'em is right at daybreak, while he's still asleep, an we got light enough'ta see what we are doin."

"Sounds good." Jason said. "Then you'll do it?"

"Now hear me out, Jason. We ain't doin it by ourselves, you got'ta help. We figure if'n you'll git up and meet us at his diggins, we'll have'em all tied up time you git there. Then we'll all take'em to the hills."

"I believe I should stay in town and…"

"Lessen we do it our way." Pecos interrupted. "It's all off."

"Okay—okay—I'll be there at daylight."

Jason got up and left. Pecos and Waco tried to hold back the laughter as they watched him go. "Us boys, is go'na show you. —Gambler man."

Waco said very facetiously before they both burst out laughing.

Dallas came up and sat down in a cane bottom chair beside Will and Carrie at the wagon. Helen and Ruth were fixing supper. Storey sat on the ground underneath the wagon unraveling some string.

"Clay will be here in'a while." Dallas said. "He'll be stayin the night here, so's to help with the team."

"Don't know how in the world you ever talked'em in'ta goin on." said Will.

"Sure will be good ta'git movin agin." said Carrie.

"Is Clays diamonds here or hid out down at his claim?" asked Dallas.

"They's in a safe place." Carrie said. "He brung'em in ever night."

"Where's they at." asked Will.

Carrie leaned over closer to them and lowered her voice.

"He's been pourin'em in'ta the water barrel round yonder on'a side of the wagon."

"Well, I'll be dogged." said Will.

Unbeknownst to the grownups, little Storey listened intently to the conversation. He became extremely frightened. His face paled, his eyes widened and his mouth opened. He began to imagine numerous ways that Clay was going to kill him. With his heart pounding he quietly slipped out from the other side of the wagon and climbed stealthily up to the water barrel. He emptied the few small stones from his pocket into the barrel and quickly climbed down. From the other side of the wagon he heard his mother call "supper time." He ran around the wagon feeling better.

"Jason! Git on up here! There's work to be done!"

Lil shouted from the saloon door to Jason as he walked slowly up the street. Jason spoke softly and sarcastically where Lil could not hear him as he smiled and waved at her.

"Yell, you loud mouth. Just wait until tomorrow. I'll be doing no more of your dirty work."

Clay arrived with his bedroll, shovel and pan. He put them down by the wagon.

"Got somthin ta'eat mama, I'm hungry as an o'bear."

"Over yonder in the pot, son." Carrie answered.

"Hey Clay, sure glad ya'changed yer mind." said Will.

"Yeah Paw, can't wait'ta git on'ta California."

"Sure pleases me ta'hear that, son."

" There's somthin needs to be talked bout." Dallas said seriously. "You know how I am bout being ready to protect myself when trouble comes. Well, now I've got more to protect, What I'm sayin is we need to be ready for any kind of trouble. We will be goin through outlaw country and Indian territory before we git to California."

They all listened intently.

" If we was to run up on an outlaw band or some renegade Indians, we would be in big trouble without means to fight them off."

"What I'm suggesting is when we git to Fort Worth, that I buy bout five carbines and plentiful shells. Then someplace between there an Abilene, we'll stop fer a day an I'll teach everbody to shoot. Also, if'n Clay wouldn't mind handling a team, I'd like'ta add one more wagon fer Helen an me an Storey—anyway, it's almost impossible to circle two wagons."

"Dallas." Will asked. "Where we go'na git the money fer all that. We sure ain't got enough."

"I've got enough in the Fort Worth bank to handle it." Dallas said. "I've got more in El Paso, and Tombstone.

"Gollee." Clay expounded. "I'll be glad to drive yer team, Dallas."

"Tell'ya what, Clay. In payment fer handlin my team. I'll git you a good ridin hoss and a saddle. —Once we git there. We best all bed down early." Dallas said. "Be a long day tomorrow."

When Clay finished eating and all had gone to their respective sleeping place. Will blew out the lantern and the camp went dark.

"We goin walkin, Dallas?"

Chapter 11

Dawn broke on the sleeping town as Jason slipped out of his tent, crept down to the street and headed south toward Clays claim. At the Summers campsite Will had started the fire and Carrie put the coffee pot over it. Ollie had hitched up his team and Clay was hitching up the Summers team.

Pecos and Waco had brought their horses up past the saloon before daylight so as to be ready to go into action at dawn. They lead their horses to the rail in front of the saloon and tied them. Pecos took eight sticks of dynamite from his saddle bags while Waco jimmied the saloon door. They both went inside.

Jason crouched down and slipped up close to Clays lean'to. He called out in a whisper.

"Pecos—Pecos—Pecos—are you there?"

Blackburn stuck his head and his shotgun out from under the front of the lean-to.

"Just one more step mister—an you're dead."

"Reverend? What are you doing here?"

"You're on my claim, mister. An like I said—one more step an you're a dead man. Now turn round an git."

Jason, still in the crouched position started backing up. Thoroughly confused, he hastily turned and left.

Most everyone still slept peacefully along the creek and hillside in their makeshift shelters, not being aware of any activity in town. And then—KABROOOOOMMMMMOOHHoommm—such a tremendous explosion occurred that it would be talked about for years to come. The explosion shook the ground and blew the entire top, front and one side from the saloon. Pecos and Wacos frightened horses broke loose from the hitching rail and ran off up the street. Pecos and Waco emerged from the saloon coughing, choking and blinded from the smoke. As they fought the smoke and tried to find their horses, Lil and the saloon girls came running out of their tent in their night robes. Lil began yelling and screaming. Pecos ran down the street and Waco around the side of the saloon. Warbuck stepped into the street and tripped Pecos. He sprawled into the street, turned over and sat up shaking his head. He looked up and saw Warbuck with his gun drawn and immediately threw his hands up and yelled.

"Don't shoot! Don't shoot!"

Warbuck looked at Pecos in disgust and motioned with his gun for him to get up. A lot of people came running up, mostly half dressed, and others were still coming. Lil continued to yell and scream. From between the tents Waco had Warbuck lined up in his shaking gun-sight as Warbuck was bringing Pecos up the street with his hands high in the air. Waco's hand shook as his thumb started to pull back the hammer of his revolver. The muzzle of a shotgun barrel pressed hard against his ear.

"Lower the gun or I'll blow yer head off." said Will.

Dallas brought Pecos up to the crowd and Will brought Waco from between the tents. Lil pointed and yelled excitedly.

"They're the diamond theives!! They're the diamond thieves!!"

"Git'em, string'em up!! They're the diamond thieves!!"

The huge mob of miners quickly became infuriated. They took Pecos and Waco as Dallas and Will turned and went across the walk bridge toward the wagons. They heard Pecos and Waco yelling "It was Jason's idea….I got religion… I'm a Christian… It was Jason's idea." They heard loud comments from the miners. "tar and feather'em….run'em out on'a rail…. string'em up."

Lil pointed down the street and yelled louder.

"There's another one of them. He's they're leader. Get'em—he's their leader. He's a diamond thief too. Get him!!!" Some of the miners looked by Lil in the direction she pointed and started running that way as others joined in. A very bewildered Jason Ransom stood in the middle of the street down past the blacksmith shop. He watched them as they ran toward him and hesitantly moved from side to side wondering what was going on and if he should run or not. He had become very frightened as the miners ran up and grabbed him. Lil was right along with them yelling about him being their leader as the miners dragged him up the street and joined the others that held Pecos and Waco. Mob justice was in order as the street was full of frenzied miners dragging Jason, Pecos and Waco up toward the end of town and yelling about what should be done. If anyone had of been interested, they could have looked around behind them and across the creek to see the Summers and Fenton wagons turned around and headed south to a pre-determined place to ford the creek with Dallas Warbuck out in front on his big red sorrel. Will, Carrie and Helen, looked out across the team from the wagon seat ecstatic with happiness.

Clay and Ruth walked along behind the Summers wagon playing tag with Storey.

As the two wagons were fording the creek, Dallas and Will looked behind them and saw Rufus hurrying to catch up, with Ol'Betsy tied up short behind the wagon. Will stood up and yelled back to him.

"Hey Rufus!! —Ya'came ta'ya senses—huh!!

Rufus waved at him as Dallas went back to help him cross the creek.

Ollie Fenton was alone on his wagon seat with a smile on his face when Mrs. Fenton poked her head out from inside the wagon.

"Ollie." she exclaimed excitedly. "There's a whole parcel of diamond pouches hid under our bed."

"Hush woman!"

Ollie frowned, and then his frown turned to a sly smile.

"That's the Lord's share."

"You're a good man, Ollie Fenton."

"A-Men!"

By the time the three wagons had crossed the creek and topped the valley rim. The bright golden morning sun, streaked through the tall pine, onto their back as they elatedly headed west. "A-Men" said Ollie.

the end

ABOUT THE AUTHOR
in a nutshell

Jim Feazell—Retired filmmaker and singer/songwriter, worked in Hollywood for twenty-two years as a motion picture and television stunt actor. After retiring from stunt work, he worked for fifteen years as a Producer, Director, Cinematographer and screenplay writer. He headed his own film company in El Dorado, Arkansas / Tucson, Arizona / and Hollywood, California. He has only recently, after retiring from motion picture production, began to write novels. This novel "The Lord's Share" is preceded by "Come The Swine" and "Dry Heat" Watch for "The Legend Of Cat Mountain" and "The Trouble With Rodney" A dual Novelette. And "Return To Heaven" A sequel to "Come The Swine."